RUTH'S WAR

It's the beginning of the war and Ruth Lewis, a teacher in Wales, befriends six-year-old evacuee Eddie Walker from London and meets Eddie's widowed father Jimmy. Later, as the war progresses, Ruth goes to London working as an ambulance driver. When Jimmy comes home injured he and Ruth have a short time together before he has to return to the fighting. Then a telegram arrives to say Jimmy is missing in action, but Ruth refuses to give up hope.

TERESA ASHBY

◆

RUTH'S WAR

Complete and Unabridged

LINFORD
Leicester

First published in Great Britain in 1992

First Linford Edition
published 2012

British Library CIP Data

Ashby, Teresa.
  Ruth's war. - -
  (Linford romance library)
  1. Wales- -Social conditions- -20th
  century- -Fiction. 2. London (England)
  - -History- -*1800 – 1950*- -Fiction.
  3. Love stories. 4. Large type books.
  I. Title II. Series
  823.9′2–dc23

  ISBN 978–1–4448–1250–3

Published by
F. A. Thorpe (Publishing)
Anstey, Leicestershire

Set by Words & Graphics Ltd.
Anstey, Leicestershire
Printed and bound in Great Britain by
T. J. International Ltd., Padstow, Cornwall

This book is printed on acid-free paper

1

'I don't want to go, Nan!'

Nell Walker froze in her tracks. Those were the very words she'd been dreading. She kept her back to the little boy and busied herself, packing his small case, not trusting herself to meet his gaze.

'I said . . . ' Eddie tried again, louder this time, thinking that perhaps she hadn't heard him or worse, was ignoring him. Nell turned around and looked down at him, sitting there on the bed, his little feet dangling way off the floor.

She'd given him such a good wash that he practically shone and he was still red behind the ears where she'd scrubbed him.

Ruffling his thick, fair hair, she smiled, she hoped, in a jolly way, for the last thing she was feeling was jolly.

''Course you do!' she announced perkily. 'You're going to the country! You'll see cows and fields and mountains. Now look, I'm putting your stuff in my own special, little case. It's the one Her Ladyship gave me!'

Keep talking, she thought, keep talking and you'll get through this! Because while you're talking, you're not thinking, not getting upset and you mustn't get upset because then Eddie'll get upset and that's the last thing you want.

He stared at her with round, blue eyes that reflected all the hurt and feelings of betrayal he must have locked up inside him. It didn't matter how many times she tried to explain to him why all this was happening, he still didn't understand.

'I don't want to go,' he said flatly.

'You're missing a button off your coat!' Nell cried, pouncing on her little wicker needlework basket. 'Sit still and I'll find another.'

It gave her something else to think

about for the last few minutes they had together. She bowed her head with its neat, grey hair over the coat and with agile fingers, quickly fastened a new button in place.

'There,' she said, snapping the thread with her teeth. 'Not quite the same, but it'll do.'

'I want to see my dad.' Eddie's little, white face was set in a grim expression.

'You will, lovey.' Nell gave him a hug.

'When?'

'Soon,' Nell promised rashly. She had no idea when. He was away, goodness knew where because she certainly didn't and if war came, then heaven only knew what would happen to him.

'Will that Mr Hitler drop his bombs on London, Nan?'

''Course he won't!' Nell cried. 'He wouldn't dare!'

'Why can't I stay here then?'

'I fell right into that one, didn't I?' Nell grinned and at last Eddie's face cracked and a smile appeared, albeit a small one. Big or small, he had a roguish smile which never failed to warm her heart.

'You're a big boy now, Eddie,' she said. 'Nearly seven! And you'll be able to write and tell me all about the countryside. It's years since I was in the country.'

She heard voices outside and went to the open window to look out at the street. Several women were hurrying along towards the school with their children.

For a moment, her heart felt close to bursting and she wanted to grab him and hold him tight and never let him go. He'd been as dear to her as her own son, since his mother had died when he was still a babe in arms. Nell was all the mum he'd ever had and sending him off into the unknown, however much they said it was for the best, was still the biggest wrench of her life.

'Ready then?' she said, picking up the battered, little case. 'Got your gas mask?'

He picked the brown box up from

the bed and pushed the string over his shoulder. The string was too long and the box almost hit his ankles.

'I'll shorten it . . . ' She went to take it, but somehow she finished up hugging him and they both began to cry.

'It'll do you good,' she kept muttering through the tears, and all the while, he was sobbing and saying, 'Don't send me away, Nan!'

It took a little while for them both to calm down, then Nell opened the door and told Eddie to mind the stairs with that gas mask dangling round his legs. The people from the neighbouring houses and the flats opposite came out into the street to say goodbye to Eddie. One old lady pushed a bar of chocolate into his tiny hand.

Nell hadn't the heart to scold him for forgetting to say thank you, but once they were among the others heading for the school, he squared his little shoulders, lifted his chin and looked ready to take on the world.

It was only a short walk to the school and Nell found herself walking so fast that Eddie was having to run to keep up. There were policemen at the school gates and dozens of women standing at the railings, trying to see their own little children through the big windows.

'Sorry, love,' one of the policemen said, putting his hand on her shoulder. 'You can't go in there.'

'Who says?' Nell bristled.

'Don't be awkward, love.'

'Best let him go in with the other kids,' a young woman advised Nell. 'It'd be best for him in the long run.'

She looked around her at the other people and realised she was one of the last to arrive. There was still time to snatch him up in her arms and run back to the house. Instead, she crouched down, even though it pained her knees to do so, and fiddled about, straightening Eddie's collar, smoothing down his coat.

When it came to saying goodbye, she couldn't do it. She didn't dare in case she started crying all over again and started him off. It didn't matter how much she told herself he'd be safer away from London, it still hurt.

So she gave him a small push that sent him forward and said nothing. She watched him go off through the gates, then the big doors of the school shut behind him and Nell found herself, with all the others, craning her neck and straining to try and see something, anything beyond those wretched windows.

Some of the bigger boys were out in the playground and Nell saw they had great big labels fastened to their coats. Labelled, like pieces of meat!

After what seemed an eternity, one of the school teachers came outside and had a word with the policemen at the gates. Nell guessed what was coming. They wanted the parents out of the way! Well, she wasn't a parent, she was a grandparent and, therefore, the rules didn't apply to her.

She was right. One of the policemen

spoke to the assembled adults.

'They're going to take the children to the tube station,' he said. 'You can stand here and wave, but don't follow them.'

Nell took off then, rushing down familiar alleys so that she would reach the tube station before the evacuees. She was puffing and panting by the time she got there and amazed to see scores of other people had beaten her to it.

She looked down the street and saw them coming in an untidy line. Her heart was thundering and when she saw Eddie, she gave out an involuntary cry.

He looked so tiny and thin and frail with her old case in one hand and his brown box slung over his other shoulder. Someone had shortened the string and now it bumped against his hip. He still clasped the bar of chocolate in his hand and Nell could see it was starting to melt.

'Eddie!' she called and he looked up, hope flashing in his eyes only to die swiftly when he realised she had only come to wave him off.

She bit her lip. Perhaps she shouldn't have come here.

'Ta, ta, Nan!' he called cheerfully and, with a gutsy little wave, he disappeared down into the tube, leaving Nell to stand there with tears pouring down her face wondering if she'd done the right thing.

The train arrived in Wales over three hours late and when the doors opened and the children began to pour out, the small crowd waiting on the platform was overwhelmed with disbelief.

There seemed so many of them and some were so young. The journey had obviously been harrowing for them, particularly the younger ones and very few were actually showing any interest at all in their new surroundings.

'We'll get them straight to the school,' one of the ladies from the WVS said, taking charge. 'The sooner these poor mites are found somewhere to stay, the better!'

The small school had never held so many children at one time and for a while, all was chaos and confusion.

Ruth Lewis had never seen anything like it in her life. The children were all so pale, many were crying and her heart went out to them. They were so young and the train journey from London was a long and arduous one. But it would be impossible to comfort all of them when weariness and misery seemed to be rife amongst them.

Even Mr Jones, the billeting officer, seemed dismayed at the spectacle. He cleared his throat and spoke to the children, gathered as they were in the school assembly hall.

'Welcome to Wales,' he began and laughed nervously. He made a small speech, but the children hardly listened. They were tired and frightened and bewildered.

The ladies of the WVS shuffled their feet, wishing he'd get on with it. They'd been planning this for months, then along came Mr Jones, with his important-sounding title of billeting officer, to take charge of things.

Placing the children took hours. One woman actually examined three or four for head lice and fleas before settling on a sturdy pair of girls. Ruth was shocked that the children were being treated almost like livestock, the strongest, healthiest and least tearful specimens being picked out quite quickly.

But was it any wonder? These people were volunteering to take unknown children into their homes for any length of time. It was a big step to take and without the kindness of people like these, goodness only knew where the children would end up.

The older children were placed in a matter of minutes, the others took longer and the longer it dragged on, the more upset the little ones got.

Ruth was a teacher at the school and would have many of the new arrivals in her class when the new term started. As the children were thinned out, she moved among them, offering words of comfort. She loved children, all children. She didn't see strength or weakness, clean or dirty, she simply saw the child.

★   ★   ★

It wasn't until after the last child had gone and Mr Jones was packing his own charges into his car that Ruth caught sight of a brown cap behind one of the benches. Thinking that one of the children had mislaid it, she hurried over to retrieve it and found not only a cap, but a child wearing it, fast asleep on the floor.

She read his label, then touched his shoulder gently.

'Eddie,' she said softly. 'Come along, Eddie, time to wake up.'

He opened his eyes, lay perfectly still for a moment, then scrambled into a sitting position and looked around in terror.

'It's all right, Eddie,' Ruth said. 'You fell asleep, that's all. Just sit there and gather your wits. I'll be right back.'

She stood up, leaving him there for a moment to collect himself and went outside to speak to Mr Jones who was preparing to drive off.

'I've just found another one,' she said. 'A little boy.'

Mr Jones looked dismayed.

'I can't take any more with me,' he said. 'I've already two more than I can manage! Can't you take him, Miss Lewis?'

'I've just my one room with Mrs Ellis,' Ruth said. 'Otherwise, I wouldn't hesitate.'

'Well, I think that just about everyone took more children than they intended,' Mr Jones muttered. 'Did Griffith Thomas turn up? He said he would, but I can't remember seeing him.'

Ruth shook her head. She would have noticed if Griffith Thomas had been there. He was a big, burly farmer with a ruddy face, topped with a thick thatch of red hair and the temper to go with it.

'Fetch him out then,' Mr Jones said.

'I'll drive by the farm and see if Griff will take him in.'

She went back inside the hall to find the little boy sitting on a bench, huddled in a corner.

'Come on, lovey,' she said and his blue eyes widened.

'That's what my nan calls me,' he said.

'Is it now?' Ruth smiled and held out her hand. The little boy hesitated, then placed his small, thin hand in hers. 'How old are you, Eddie?'

'Nearly seven,' he said, rubbing a grimy hand across his face and leaving a dirty smear. Most of the children had arrived dirty, hardly surprising when they had been crammed in a hot, filthy train for hours.

'Nearly seven, eh?' she said. 'You'll be in my class here at the school then!'

He gazed up at her and his fingers tightened around her hand.

'Sometimes, when the weather's fine, we have lessons outside. Did you ever do that in London, Eddie?'

He shook his head.

Once outside, he looked about him and pressed close against Ruth. She squeezed his hand reassuringly. To a child from the city, the dramatic landscape here must seem as completely alien as the noise and bustle of the city would be to a local child.

'Hurry, Miss Lewis!' Mr Jones called from his car and Eddie gripped Ruth's hand with both his and stared up at her, panic stricken.

No wonder. Mr Jones was becoming impatient and it showed in his tone of voice. He didn't care much for children and had five of them bouncing around in the back of his highly-treasured car.

'I'll take him up,' Ruth said. 'You've enough to do!'

For the first time all day, Mr Jones actually smiled, even if it was a little rueful.

'I don't know what Mrs Jones is going to say,' he said before driving off.

'I'm going to take you to stay with Mr Thomas,' Ruth explained to Eddie as they set off along the road. 'He's a farmer and as long as you're helpful and polite, I'm sure that you and he will get along.'

'Can't I stay with you, miss?' Eddie whispered.

'I'm afraid not, lovey. You'll be all right with Mr Thomas.'

Mr Thomas was rough and ready, a little surly and prone to fits of temper, but Ruth knew he was a decent sort and the boy certainly wouldn't want for anything or come to any harm with him.

'Shall I carry that for you?' She held out her hand and took the shabby, little case. It was quite light, but would be feeling heavy to a tired, little boy.

Eddie stopped and looked about him. He'd seen pictures of hills and mountains in books, but it didn't prepare him for this. The hills were so steep, but lush and green and spotted with white sheep.

'Haven't you ever been to the country before, Eddie?'

'No,' he mumbled.

'You'll like it.' She laughed. 'I lived in London for a few years and I loved it, but it's very different here.'

'You lived in London?' He seized on this almost as though it were a lifeline.

'Yes, I did.' She smiled. 'I went to live there when I was ten and stayed there until I left school!'

Actually, she knew quite well how Eddie must be feeling. When her parents died and she was sent to live in London with her mother's second cousin, she had felt so lost and alone. She'd never forget the feeling of despair when she arrived in that busy city and saw an ocean of strange faces. She'd been wearing a label, too, pinned to her coat and clutching a small bag containing all her belongings.

Then suddenly, a woman had detached herself from the crowds, a big woman with white hair dressed entirely in black and Ruth could remember thinking fearfully, Please God, don't let this be her . . .

But it was cousin Rachel and beneath that fearsome veneer had beat a heart of pure gold. She'd taken Ruth under her wing and to her heart and had given her the soundest base upon which to rebuild her shattered life. She'd been at college when cousin Rachel died and had been unable to face London again, so instead, had returned to take up teaching in Wales.

They began to walk on. It was quite a way to Thomas's farm, but it wouldn't do Eddie any harm to stretch his legs.

'This is a nice case,' she said.

'It's my nan's,' Eddie said. 'She had it when she was in service. She used to work in a lordship's house and sometimes, the ladyship would go off to Kent and take the servants with her!'

'A real lordship.' Ruth smiled. 'Good gracious!'

'In the Great War, Nan used to hear the battles in France and see the fires! My grandad was a soldier. My dad's going to be a soldier if there's a war, he told me so!'

Once he got going, Eddie was quite a bright, chirpy boy and Ruth enjoyed his company as they walked along the lane which wound tightly uphill. By the time they reached Thomas's farm, she had been told Eddie's life history. She knew all about his mother dying when he was a baby and his nan raising him in her house in the East End of London.

He painted quite a vivid picture and although she was never likely to meet her, Ruth knew that she would like Eddie's nan.

They turned off the lane and there was the farmhouse. It was a white, stone building beneath a grey, slate roof and in front of it was a yard where hens roamed freely.

Eddie looked around, seeing dogs, cats and a pig wandering around or just laying asleep in the last patch of sunlight.

'Why don't the dogs eat the chickens?' Eddie whispered.

'They just don't.' Ruth shrugged. 'I

don't think it would even cross their minds.'

She felt Eddie pull back slightly as she led him to the back door of the house, then the door was flung open and a huge man filled the doorway.

Eddie shrank back behind Ruth. He'd never seen a man so big, or so frightening.

'You said you might take an evacuee, Mr Thomas,' Ruth said.

'Today was it?' Griffith Thomas rubbed his huge paw of a hand through his unruly red hair. 'Well, what have you got for me? Let me see.'

Ruth gently pushed Eddie into view and the huge man towered over the small child.

'He's a bit thin,' he said.

'He's only six,' Ruth said.

'He'll do,' he said, not cracking his face. 'What's his name?'

'Eddie,' Ruth Lewis said. 'Eddie Walker. And I shall expect to see him at school on Monday.'

2

Sunday, September 3, 1939, was a warm, sunny day and Nell Walker had taken a chair into the street in order to soak up the last of the summer sunshine before the long, dreary nights of winter set in. There was a strange feeling in the air, of anticipation and dread and Nell knew, as sure as sure, that the country would have to go to war. It gave her a strange kind of tingle every time she thought about it.

She pulled a thread of wool from a bag and her needles worked furiously. She was making a sweater for Eddie for the winter and wanted it ready to send to him as soon as she heard where he'd been billeted.

'Nell!'

She looked up and saw someone waving to her from one of the flats opposite.

'Are you going to come up and listen to the wireless?'

'No,' Nell said. 'No, I'd rather sit out here.'

Everyone had gone in to listen to Mr Chamberlain's speech, but Nell doubted he'd be saying anything she wanted to hear.

It all came back to her as she sat there with the sun warming her face, the long, dark days of the Great War when her own Eddie, little Eddie's grandfather, had been a soldier fighting at the Somme. Things had been different then, but people were still people and young men would still die. She shivered, feeling oddly cold. Surely fate wouldn't be cruel enough to take Jimmy?

Ever since the talk of war started, he'd been going on about joining up. She doubted he'd wait for his call-up papers. For all she knew, he might already be in uniform and preparing to fight. The Territorials had already been mobilised.

Right now, she wasn't sure where her son was. For the past few months, he'd been coming and going, sometimes staying away for weeks at a stretch. Whenever she asked what he was up to, he'd just grin and say he'd been working.

But working at what? It worried her. He'd been a bright boy at school and the teachers said he would go far, but he'd always been restless and had never settled down to anything. The awful thing was that she knew a war would probably be the making of him — or the death of him, one of the two.

She wasn't sure she could go through it all again, the waiting, the wondering, the fear. Seeing all those broken-up young men arriving in droves at the station, some of them missing limbs, others blinded or injured so badly they didn't even know who they were.

Her Ladyship had insisted on joining in with the voluntary efforts and had taken Nell along with her. She'd seen things then, in her young life, that she'd prayed with all her heart she'd never have to see again. And now the streets were full of brave, young men ready once again to go to war and one of them was her one and only son.

He'd been just a baby in the last war, living the life of Riley, running around with the children of nobility. It had done him good, made him bold and unafraid. He could hold his own in any situation and was as comfortable talking to a lord as anyone else.

'Mum . . . '

Blinded by the sun as she looked up, she saw only a dark shape towering over her chair, but there was only one person in the world who could call her 'Mum.' Her knitting fell to the ground, forgotten in her excitement, as she got to her feet and hugged her son.

'I thought you'd be home before this,' she said reproachfully, noting that he wasn't wearing a uniform yet and feeling secretly pleased that it was so.

His strong arms lifted her up and spun her round and when he set her down, she had her back to the sun and time to study him.

'You're thinner,' she said. 'And you need a haircut! What have you been doing? Where have you been to get all brown like that?'

'Glad to see you, too, Mum!' He laughed.

He had a broad grin, a cheerful face altogether which dimpled when he smiled and blue eyes that were always sparkling. She'd only once seen the sparkle vanish and that was when his young wife had died.

'Where's the nipper?' He shoved his hands in his pockets and looked up and down the road where the kids usually played on a Sunday (so long as they'd been to Sunday school).

'He . . . he's gone,' she said, blinking. 'Most of the kids went.'

'You didn't . . . ' He gasped. 'Tell me you're joking, Mum! Not our Eddie . . . he's just a little lad.'

'It's not going to be safe here,' she said. 'And you weren't here, so I had to make the decision.'

'I've been working!' he said. 'I got back as quick as I could. Where has he gone?'

'Wales,' Nell said, picking up her knitting.

'Where in Wales?'

She turned away from him.

'They'll let us know . . . '

'Mum!' Jimmy shouted. 'I want to see him before I join up! How can I do that when you don't know where he's gone?'

'I did what I thought was best,' Nell repeated. 'It wasn't easy letting him go.'

Despite herself, she felt the tears well in her eyes and begin to run in streams down her face.

'Poor little scrap,' she cried. 'What else was I supposed to do?'

In the distance, they heard the striking of the hour. It was eleven o'clock.

'I'm sorry, Mum,' Jimmy put his arm around her and squeezed her tight. 'Don't cry, love. You were right. He'll

26

be better off out of it once it starts —
and so would you. You did the right
thing — I don't know what came over
me to go off at you like that.'

'It can't not start now, can it, Jim?'
Nell said fearfully.

Next door, a window was thrown
open.

'Nell . . . Yoo hoo! Nell!

Nell and Jimmy looked round.

'It's on the wireless!' the beaming
face at the window called excitedly
down to her. 'We're at war!'

★   ★   ★

Ruth Lewis trembled. What on earth
would happen now?

It amazed her the different ways in
which people had taken the news. Some
were quite calm and philosophical
about it all, others were joyful and
excited while yet more were sunk into
the pits of gloom. She wasn't even sure
which category she herself fitted into.
Would the war even reach out as far as

the valley? Would it ever come to that? In some ways it was a relief to know that the waiting was over at last.

She trembled again and looked out across the steep hills. If only there were some way of looking into the future. A few feet away, Richard Noble lay on his back staring up at the sky. He wasn't a native of Wales, but his mother had come from Cardiff and so he claimed to be half Welsh by birthright.

He was a strange man. Tall and thin with a long, narrow nose and brown eyes, his mouth was wide and his teeth white which gave him the appearance of a movie star. He was a teacher at the boys' council school a few miles from her own and they'd had something of a relationship for the past year or so.

'I may join the RAF,' he said, propping himself up on one elbow and gazing up at her. 'I don't see myself as a foot soldier!'

She'd heard it all before. Richard spoke grandly about what he'd do and what he wouldn't do, but Ruth knew deep down in her heart that he wouldn't willingly leave the valley.

'You may not need to go,' she said. 'Being a teacher — '

'With flat feet!' He held up one huge foot and laughed throatily. 'They'll take anyone, Ruth. Anyone fit enough to fight.'

There was a note of bitterness in his voice which Ruth picked up on straight away.

'There's no shame in not wanting to kill your fellow man, Richard,' she said and his face darkened.

'I didn't say that,' he said and they lapsed into an uneasy silence. She looked at the back of his head. He was still watching the skies and she knew he was imagining himself up there in the clouds, a fighter pilot. In his own imagination, Richard was ready to do anything, but in real life . . .

There was no way of knowing what went on in his mind. Despite the fact that they'd been so close for a year, she felt she hardly knew him at all. In fact, lately she had begun to wonder if he really knew himself.

He turned around and smiled at her.

'Anyway,' he said. 'it'll probably be over in a month or two.'

'Let's hope so,' she said, but didn't really believe it anymore than he did.

'Ruth, if I do get called up — if I do have to go away — '

He stopped and began to tear grass out by the roots, his knuckles white. She waited.

'Will you marry me before I go?' He looked directly into her eyes and she tried to meet his gaze, but her eyes fell despite herself.

'Do I take it the answer's no?' he said.

'Richard, I . . . '

'Would it make any difference to your feelings if I were wearing a uniform?'

'You don't know me at all to say something like that!'

'Don't answer yet. Think about it. It's just . . . it'd be so much easier being away if I knew you were here waiting for me.'

She stared in horror at the grass. What could she say to him? How could she promise to marry him when she wasn't sure that she loved him? And he'd never said he loved her, not once, not even hinted at it.

'We've been going out for a year now,' he went on quickly. 'We would have married eventually anyway.'

'Would we?' She looked up at him.

He shrugged. 'I expect so, don't you?'

'I don't know, Richard,' she said softly. She cared for him, but love? As for spending the rest of her life with him, she wasn't at all sure she wanted to.

'I mean, I'll probably die anyway if they send me away,' he said.

'Don't say that!'

'Why?' His eyes teased. 'Does it upset you?'

'Of course it does,' she said.

'Then think about marrying me, Ruth . . . please.'

'I'll think about it, Richard,' she promised and when she looked up at him, he was smiling the triumphant smile of the victorious.

★   ★   ★

Eddie stood beside the bed, tears streaming down his face. There was a huge, wet patch on the under sheet and his pyjamas were sticking wetly to his legs. He couldn't believe it had happened. It was the kind of thing little children did, not big boys like him.

He rammed his fist into his mouth to stop himself from crying out loud. He'd been woken up by the cock crowing, then the clopping of feet in the yard as Griffith Thomas herded the cows out to graze after milking.

The big man hadn't said much and what he did say Eddie had difficulty in understanding. He'd been looking forward to his first day at school, perhaps to seeing some familiar faces and especially to seeing Miss Lewis again.

It had been on the radio the day before about the war. Griffith Thomas had sat in silence listening to the Prime Minister's broadcast with tears rolling down his ruddy face. He hadn't even bothered to hide them. Eddie had been puzzled. He'd never seen a man crying before, except when Mr Balfry from the corner shop came out of the pub of a Friday night, howling his eyes out and waking the whole of the street!

'What's this then?'

He spun round, startled, his eyes popping. The farmer had come into his room and must now be able to see the damning evidence! He walked over to the bed and looked down at the stain, then turned to look at the child.

'Oh, dear,' he said and clicked his tongue. 'I'll get some water on to heat so you can have a wash,' he said.

Eddie flinched. He'd been expecting a shout of anger at the very least, at worst . . . a beating.

He realised he was shaking, from head to toe and his teeth were chattering. But he wasn't cold, not cold at all.

Griffith Thomas frowned, his forehead turning to a sea of wavy lines.

'There now,' he said, his voice shockingly gentle for a man so huge. 'Don't mind that. I'll wash the bed down while you're at school and put it out to dry.'

Still Eddie shook.

'Come on, boy.' Griffith held out his arms awkwardly. 'No harm done . . . '

Eddie took a tentative step towards him, then the big man picked him up, not minding his wet pyjamas and held him tight, soothing him with kind words in a language Eddie didn't understand.

The tears and the trembling finally subsided and Griffith Thomas put the boy down.

'Now hear me, boy. You come downstairs and have a good wash down and get ready for school.' His face was stern again, his manner abrupt.

Then he hurried out, his feet clomping on the bare stairs as he went down to the kitchen and, with a shaky sigh, Eddie followed him.

3

It had been a week and most of the children seemed to have found their feet . . . and their tongues!

The class had doubled in size and Ruth Lewis had little, pale sparrows from London, sitting alongside the bonny, tanned youngsters from the village and its surrounds. Little Gwennie Edwards had taken Eddie Walker under her wing and all seemed to be well there.

They were like foreigners to each other though. Most of the children in her class had never been beyond the valleys, while the majority of the Londoners had never set foot outside the city. They even had trouble understanding each other and were constantly mimicking each other's accents.

They were all silent at the moment,

arms folded, backs straight, waiting for her to begin reading to them. She looked around at the sea of faces. They'd settled in so quickly, the little strangers. One or two were still prone to fits of the miseries, but that was only to be expected under the circumstances.

She took a deep breath, ready to start reading, when there was a loud rap at the classroom door.

'Excuse me,' she said and hurried to the door.

'Can you come, Miss Lewis?' the girl said. 'You're wanted in Mr Barker's room.'

'Thank you,' Ruth said. 'Tell Mr Barker that I'll be right along.'

She turned to speak to the class, appointed two of the more sensible children to take turns reading aloud to the others and hurried to the headmaster's office. Surely they weren't to expect more evacuees?

'Come in, Miss Lewis,' Mr Barker responded to her knock.

She entered the room and went straight to his desk.

'You wanted to speak to me?' she said.

'About Eddie Walker,' the headmaster said. 'He is in your class, isn't he?'

'Yes, sir.'

'Would you mind letting him out for an hour or so? Only his father has come all the way from London to — '

She turned around, suddenly aware that there was someone else in the room.

A tall, thin man with wide shoulders, who could only be Eddie's father, stood in one corner of the head's office, hat in hand. Yet he looked so young. He turned around and grinned at her, his eyes crinkling and she felt her face flush with hot colour.

'This is Mr Walker, Eddie's father.' Mr Barker came out from behind his desk to formally introduce them.

Jimmy Walker held out his hand and took Ruth's in a firm, business-like shake.

'Sorry to just turn up like this, Miss Lewis,' he said. 'But I'm soon to be posted overseas and I wanted to see the nipper . . . I don't know when I'll next get the chance.'

'Of course.' Ruth mentally shook herself and returned his friendly smile. But she couldn't shake off the feeling that this man had something . . . something very special. Charisma, charm? She couldn't put her finger on it, but felt sure whatever it was had its roots in his smile . . . or perhaps it was his sparkling, blue eyes.

If only Richard's smile had that effect on her! Then surely all her problems would be at an end.

'Is he all right?' he asked as they hurried along the school corridors. 'Settling down, I mean? Is he with a nice family?'

'He's staying on a farm,' Ruth said. 'And yes, he seems to be settling down quite well.'

She smiled, thinking back to the first day at school when Griffith Thomas had brought the boy in himself in the back of a wagon. He'd patted Eddie on the head, handed him a sandwich for his lunch and gone off, redder in the face than ever.

She opened the door of the classroom and all the children looked up. Eddie saw at once his father standing behind the teacher and jumped to his feet, his peaky, little face flooding with colour.

'Dad!' he yelled, pushing his way through the other pupils. 'Dad!'

Ruth stood to one side as Eddie tore past and flung himself at his father. Jimmy Walker swept the little boy up into his arms with no apparent effort. A lump formed in her throat as she watched their reunion. They just clung to each other in silent greeting. Softly, she closed the door and, turning to face the children, smiled, but did not trust herself to speak.

Instead, she nodded at one of the girls who, stiltedly, began to read aloud.

She slipped into her seat and closed

her eyes, but her thoughts were far removed from the book being read. She was thinking sadly, of families torn apart by war, of men who would go away and never return, of children here and now who might never be able to go home. And she thought of Richard and wondered if she could ever be the wife he deserved.

School had finished for the day when Jimmy Walker returned with his son. Ruth looked up, saw him and her breath caught in her throat. She was attracted to him, she couldn't deny that and felt that she was betraying Richard by her feelings.

'I lost track of the time.' He smiled apologetically. 'I'm sorry. I really meant to return him in time to finish his lessons.'

'That's all right,' she said. 'Did you show your dad around the village, Eddie?'

Eddie, holding tight to his father's hand, nodded vigorously.

'I've been to the farm,' Jimmy said.

'Griffith Thomas seems a good sort. Eddie likes him anyway.' He frowned, puzzled.

The man had seemed dour and surly to Jimmy, yet little Eddie's eyes had sparkled with affection when he spoke of him. He'd even made friends with the dogs and cats that seemed to be everywhere. Eddie Walker, who'd never cared for anything with fur in his life!

Jimmy looked at the school teacher and thought how different she was to the old biddies who taught Eddie in London. Ruth Lewis had brown hair, swept back in a knot and dark brown eyes as warm as chocolate. Her skin was flawless and pale. He wouldn't be at all surprised if Eddie didn't fall a little in love with her, as little boys sometimes do when faced with such beauty for the first time in their lives.

In fact, if he wasn't about to go to war himself . . . He laughed out loud at the thought, startling Ruth.

'I wish we'd met in better times,' he

said by way of explanation, his expression becoming serious, but retaining its humour.

'It might be over soon,' she said.

He didn't think so, but he didn't want to say in front of Eddie. Anyway, he shouldn't be thinking of romance, not when he was about to go to war. But perhaps when it was all over . . .

'Griff Thomas has invited me to stay overnight,' he said. 'I'll get the first train out tomorrow.'

At least, the burly farmer had grunted, 'There's a spare bed if you want it. You'd be welcome.'

'We're going to spend the evening together,' Eddie announced proudly. 'I'm taking my dad up the mountain.'

Ruth looked alarmed.

'You will be careful,' she said. 'There are some old mine workings — '

'Why don't you come along with us?' Jimmy suggested. 'You can make sure we don't fall down any holes!'

'Well, I — '

'Go on, miss! Please! You can take us

up to that bit where the river runs right through the mountain and you can look down at it!'

Ruth looked at Eddie and nodded.

'I'd like that,' she said.

She found Jimmy Walker quite fascinating. He hardly talked of the war at all and preferred to speak of mundane things. There was none of Richard's indecision here. This man had made up his mind what to do and was doing it without fuss or nonsense.

Then she felt guilty for even thinking it. It was wrong to compare Richard with Jimmy, not to mention disloyal.

'What do you do for a living?' she asked and for the first time, she saw Jimmy Walker's face darken.

'This and that,' he said eventually.

'Your parents were in service, so Eddie tells me,' she said.

'That's right.' He grinned, relaxing. 'I was raised in a huge, manor house in Kent! When Her Ladyship died, she was very generous to her staff — left my father enough to buy his own house and set up a small business!'

'Don't you carry on your father's business?' Ruth asked.

'I've had little to do with it in recent years. We've got a manager in. It's just a small garage. Maybe, when the war's over, I'll see about expanding it, but . . . '

He shrugged.

'There's no sense making plans with things as they are. Just take each day as it comes. How about you, Miss Lewis . . . ?'

'Ruth!' she exclaimed. 'We're not at school, now!'

'Ruth.' He grinned.

'I suppose I'll stay here,' she said. 'I've a small house in London, but it's been standing empty for so long, it's probably derelict by now. I . . . I just haven't been able to face going back there since my cousin died.'

'You lived in London, Ruth?'

'Yes, for several years,' she said and found herself telling this stranger all about Cousin Rachel.

'You must know something of what Eddie's feeling,' Jimmy murmured. 'I had a wonderful childhood, secure and happy. I hate to see his being all carved up like this! It was bad enough losing his mother . . . '

'I know,' Ruth said. 'But we'll do our best to make his stay here a happy one. He's already settling in well.'

They sat on the hillside, watching Eddie play, talking about everything but the war until the sun finally sank behind the mountains leaving behind a dull, red glow.

'We should go,' Ruth said, getting to her feet. 'It'll get dark pretty quickly now. I'll walk back to the farm with you.'

'Then I'll walk you home,' Jimmy said. 'You shouldn't be wandering around on your own in the dark.'

Ruth laughed. 'This isn't London!'

'I know that,' Jimmy said ruefully. 'I'll still walk you home though.'

They saw Eddie home to bed, then walked down to the village where Ruth had a room with Mrs Ellis.

'Well.' Jimmy grinned when they reached the gate. 'This is goodbye then.' He held out his hand and shook Ruth's with a formality that was oddly touching.

'I hope to see you again sometime.'

'Oh, I hope so,' Ruth said so meaningfully that her face flooded with red-hot colour. 'I mean, I hope you'll be all right.'

'Take care,' he said softly and as he turned to go, Ruth called him back.

'I'll bring Eddie down to wave you off in the morning!' she suggested, surprising herself.

'Would you?' His blue eyes positively lit up.

'I'd like to,' she said. 'I'll see you tomorrow.'

The following morning, before school started, Ruth met Jimmy and Eddie and walked down to the station with them. Eddie was subdued now, a far cry from the bouncy, joyful little boy of yesterday.

There were some young men on the

platform, some in uniform, some not, but all going to war. With them, mothers, girlfriends, wives and children waited to wave their loved ones off.

Although last goodbyes had been said, when the train pulled in, they were said again and again. Jimmy gathered his son up in his arms and hugged him and Ruth was shocked to see tears wet on Jimmy's face.

There was no embarrassment as he rubbed the tears away with his hand and again Ruth was touched by something so special, she couldn't begin to name it.

'Goodbye, Miss Lewis,' he held out his hand.

'Ruth,' she said. 'I'm Ruth, remember?' She placed her hand in his.

'Ruth,' he said her name as though relishing it and for a moment, his eyes locked with hers and she felt her head start to spin. Both realised they were still holding hands at the same time and laughed.

She put her arms around Eddie and

drew him close and gradually, she felt the tension ease out of his body as he relaxed against her.

The whistle blew and realising they had run out of time, he kissed her cheek before leaping aboard the train which was already so packed there was standing room only.

The train snaked out of the station and Ruth lifted Eddie up so he could wave until his father's waving hand was just one of many in the distance, then he turned his face against her shoulder and began to cry.

'Don't be sad, lovey,' she said softly as she carried him off the station platform. 'Your dad will come back. I know he will.'

She touched her cheek where his lips had brushed against her skin. And she hoped, with all her heart and soul, that she was right and knew that she would never marry Richard, could never marry him.

* * *

By December, all the young men had gone from the area.

Ruth watched as Richard wrestled with his conscience. He was torn in two, not wanting to fight in a war and not wanting to stay home where people were already muttering darkly about his presence.

'I'm going to join up,' he said quietly. 'And I'll ask you again, Ruth. Will you marry me?'

She looked away abruptly, her head bowed.

'Haven't you thought about it?' he said angrily, turning her head round so that she had to look at him.

'I . . . I can't marry you, Richard,' she said. 'I'm so sorry.'

'But I'm going to war!' he cried. 'I may never come back!'

'That's no reason for getting married,' Ruth said. She'd already seen it happen to others she knew. People rushing into marriage, frightened into accepting proposals and she understood that, but couldn't do it.

'What do you want?' he said, a muscle twitching at his temple. 'Love? Romance? You know me, Ruth! I can't change the way I am.'

'And I can't change the way I am,' she replied, closing her eyes so she didn't have to look at him anymore. She couldn't bear to see the pain in his eyes.

When she opened them again, he'd gone.

It was three days before she saw him again. He came to see her at the school, something he'd never done before. He was so dedicated a teacher that to him, it was almost sacrilegious to interrupt lessons.

She left her class to themselves and went to speak to him in the corridor, thinking that he had come to say goodbye.

His face was white with shock and for a moment, she thought he was going to tell her that he was to be sent overseas.

'They turned me down,' he said, his voice stilted with disbelief. 'They turned me down, Ruth.'

'Why?'

'My heart.' He touched his chest, his voice incredulous. 'It's my heart.'

'Oh, Richard — '

'And I don't know how to take it,' he said, shaking his head. 'At first I felt relieved, then disappointed now . . . My heart, Ruth! Can you believe that? They said it was something to do with the rheumatic fever I had as a child.'

'We still need men at home, Richard,' she said, touching his hair as she might a small child's.

'There's nothing here for me, Ruth,' he said bitterly. 'Nothing.'

'I'm here, Richard,' she said softly.

'Are you?' He looked at her, his eyes cold. 'Are you, Ruth? I sometimes wonder.'

⋆ ⋆ ⋆

France wasn't all it had been cracked up to be and Jimmy had experienced a strange kind of melancholy when he first set foot on French soil, remembering his father's tales of the battle of the Somme, when tens of thousands of men had perished in a matter of days.

At twenty-five, Eddie Walker was one of the older men to fight at the Somme, the same age, Jimmy reflected, as he himself was now. He'd been two at the time of the battle and hadn't known his father when he'd finally come home.

His face had worn that weary, haunted look until his death in 1930. He'd never been able to live comfortably with the fact that he'd survived the terrible carnage when so many others, his friends included, had not.

Jimmy was moving along the road from Belgium with refugees and when he saw the British troops approaching, he broke away and sought out an officer.

'You're English?' the major said in astonishment. 'What on earth are you doing with a bunch of refugees?'

'I've been behind enemy lines,' Jimmy said tiredly. 'You'll be turned back before long. There's no point in you going on — '

The major laughed in his face.

'Why should I believe you? Have you any proof of identity?'

'No,' Jimmy said. 'But if you can get on your radio, I'll tell you who to speak to and what my code-name is.'

'You're not wearing a uniform,' the major said, tugging at Jimmy's shirt. 'You know what that means if you're caught?'

'I'm aware of that.'

'I'll check you out, then we'll sort out something for you to wear! You'd better stick with us for the time being — unless, of course, you've somewhere to go?'

'I've achieved what I came here for,' Jimmy said. 'Now they'll give me a uniform and a gun and I'll fight along with the rest of you.'

'Spy?' the major said.

'Saboteur.' Jimmy grinned. 'Been at it some months now, backwards and forwards. I'm good at languages, good with machines and I know how to keep my head down. If I pick up some helpful information on the way, then I suppose that could make me a spy of sorts!

'I've been no more than a nuisance, if that, but our Government seems to believe that people like me are helpful.'

The major grinned.

Later, (it had taken three hours for the confirmation to come through) he introduced himself formally to Jimmy Walker.

'David Anderson,' he said. 'It seems you were wrong about us turning back. Our orders are to push forward to the front.'

'They'll change,' Jimmy said certainly.

He rode in a truck beside the major and noted a certain atmosphere among the men.

They were all young, keen to get on with the job they'd come to do. The sooner it was done, the sooner they'd be back home with their loved ones.

The convoy moved slowly and Jimmy was deep in thought, not seeing the French countryside going by, not joining in with the singing of the lads in the back, but letting his mind stray . . .

Not home to London, but to a distant Welsh valley where Eddie would be experiencing his first spring in the country, far, far away from the horrors of war, safe, nestling in that peaceful, little haven.

And he couldn't bring Eddie to mind without thinking, too, of the pretty, young school teacher with her shiny, brown hair and chocolate-brown eyes. As long as he knew she'd be there for Eddie, he wouldn't worry about him. He'd even written to her . . .

They passed through a village which still bore the scars of the last war and people flooded from the cottages and houses, eager hands holding out gifts of chocolate and cigarettes, the young and the not-so-young women running up to kiss some of the men on foot.

'We're in the wrong place here!' Jimmy laughed.

'We'll get ours when we've won!' someone yelled from the back of the truck and a cheer went up. It was the same in the next village and the next.

Then they ran into some more refugees, just a few at first, kids and belongings piled in and on top of cars, wagons and anything else they'd been able to lay their hands on. Women pulled carts laden with furniture and as the crowds thickened, so the vehicles became more and more strange.

At one place, the road was blocked. Traffic had come to a standstill. Jimmy climbed down from the truck and walked ahead with some of the others to investigate.

There was nothing beaten or defeated about the family at the root of the hold up. They had a small child perched up on the top of a cart and all were laughing and singing.

'What is it?' one of the soldiers asked. 'What's going on?'

'It's the little girl's birthday,' Jimmy said and automatically reached in his pocket for the chocolate he'd collected on the journey. He stepped forward and gave it to the little girl who said nothing, but who grinned a happy grin in thanks.

Then Major David Anderson took charge, asking the people to move on.

'We've a war to-go to,' he said to the men who had put up a token protest. 'With any luck, this little girl will have a lot more birthdays to celebrate!'

Back in the truck, Jimmy couldn't get the child out of his mind.

'It's the twenty-fourth of May isn't it?' he said suddenly, remembering. 'It's my boy's seventh birthday.'

Eddie's seventh birthday and there was Jimmy, on his way to the front. He wondered if there'd be a party for Eddie, presents . . . It was unlikely with things as they were and so many children.

4

'Happy birthday, Eddie!' Ruth said and the children around the table cheered. Griffith Thomas stepped forward with a jug of something fizzy which he swore wasn't in the least little bit alcoholic and filled the children's cups.

'One more drink, then you can all go home,' he said. He'd been good to put up with the children as long as he had, Ruth reflected. He wasn't known for his love of children and had preferred to live in splendid isolation since his wife had gone off ten years or so before, taking their three young children with her.

It was virtually unheard of for a woman to go off like that, especially one with the responsibility of three little ones, but that's just what Mrs Thomas had done and it had set the whole valley off gossiping for years since.

Griffith had been broken-hearted, but since little Eddie's arrival, Ruth had noticed a distinct change.

Some people said his wife had gone with another man, but only Griff knew the truth of that. Ruth did know that he possessed a certificate to say he was divorced from his wife, but the grounds were unknown. Desertion, adultery? It didn't matter. She'd gone and he was alone, but not lonely anymore.

The noise in the big, farmhouse kitchen rose to fever pitch as shrill, cockney voices did their level best to outdo the Welsh ones.

The knock at the door went almost unheard.

'Quiet!' Ruth shouted and gradually the noise subsided so that she could hear again that tentative knock.

'I'll see to it, Mr Thomas,' she said.

'I hope it's not more children,' he muttered.

The woman standing outside, smartly, but rather dowdily dressed, was holding a large handbag with both hands. Her hair was prematurely grey, but Ruth estimated that she was probably in her mid forties.

'Yes, can I help you?' Ruth said. The woman had come a long way off the road if she was lost.

'Hello,' she said, a nervous smile touching her lips but not her eyes. 'I was told I'd find Mr Thomas here.'

'That's right.' Ruth smiled warmly.

'I think.' The woman swallowed nervously. 'I mean, I was led to believe . . .'

She peered in through the open door, looked past Ruth and saw the children gathered around the huge plank table.

She gasped and there was a scream from inside the kitchen, then Eddie came belting out, flinging himself into her arms.

'Nan!' he yelled. 'What are you doing here? It's my birthday today and I'm having a party!'

'I know, lovey,' she said, tears rolling down her face. 'That's why I came to see you. Couldn't let your seventh birthday pass without seeing you.'

She hugged him and lifted him up.

'Gawd!' she groaned. 'You've put on some weight! And just look at you, how you've grown since September. And you've lost a couple of teeth, too!'

'Yes.' Eddie grinned gappily and shoved his finger against his gum. 'And the new ones are coming!'

She put Eddie down and turned to look at Ruth.

'You must be the school teacher,' she said, her smile wary. 'My Jim's told me about you.'

'Oh.' Ruth flushed.

'He's abroad . . . ' Nell's voice tailed off shyly.

'I know,' Ruth admitted. 'You must miss him.'

Griffith Thomas appeared beside them, looking from one to the other, then he smiled a rare smile and held out his hand to Nell.

'You must be Mrs Walker,' he said. 'You got my letter then?'

'Yes, I did, Mr Thomas.' She smiled

and stepped into the farmhouse. 'It was very kind of you to send for me. Very kind.'

Despite seeing Eddie again, she couldn't help noticing the warmth of Griffith Thomas's golden eyes. She'd already learned of his kind and gentle nature from his letters, but she found his size awesome.

He wrote to her regularly with news of Eddie and his last letter had contained an invitation to come and stay in Wales for a while, to celebrate Eddie's seventh birthday.

'Come an' sit down, Nan!' Eddie invited, holding a chair ready.

'You sent for her?' Ruth whispered incredulously.

Griffith's cheeks reddened.

'I've been corresponding with Eddie's nan, keeping her up to date . . . When my children went, I had nothing and I thought it might help her to know how he was getting on.

'She'll just be staying a day or so,' he said. 'I invited her to stay until . . . well, until it's over, but she won't leave London.'

Ruth nodded and looked over towards the table. Mrs Walker was watching her closely, her fixed expression giving nothing away except perhaps a little concern.

'Oh, Miss Lewis, I nearly forgot! Eddie got a letter from his father,' Griffith said, going over to the vast mantel shelf. 'There was one inside it for you.'

Ruth's hand shook as she took it and pushed it into her pocket.

'I'll read it later,' she said, embarrassed.

'Will you walk these children home now?' Griffith said.

'Of course,' Ruth said and clapped her hands to bring the children to order. When they'd all got their coats and said their thank-yous and good-byes, Ruth turned to speak to Mrs Walker.

'It was nice to meet you,' she said politely. 'If you've time, why don't you

64

come by the school and see Eddie's work?'

'I'd like that.' Nell Walker smiled and lost years off her age. She wasn't being deliberately off-hand, she was simply shy and a little unsure of herself in strange surroundings.

'I should thank you, too,' she went on. 'For your letters telling me about Eddie. It made it all much more bearable.'

Griffith looked puzzled.

'You've both been very kind.' Nell smiled. 'I don't know what I'd have done without your letters . . .'

'I'm glad.' Ruth smiled and herding the children together like a bunch of cackling hens, set off down the road.

'I'll help you with all this washing up,' Nell declared, rolling back her sleeves, but Griffith put up his hands.

'Eddie, take your nan into the front room. You'll have plenty to talk about.'

'But, I —'

'I've been doing the washing up around here for the past ten years on my own,' Griffith said abruptly. 'I've my own way of doing things and I don't intend to change. Besides, you're a guest in my house.'

Nell, knowing when she was beaten, smiled and let Eddie lead her through to the living room. It was small compared to the huge kitchen, but cosy and inviting.

She sat down in a big, fireside chair and held out her arms.

'Now come and sit on my knee and tell me what you've been doing to look so bonny!'

Eddie scrambled on to her lap and put his arms around her neck. He didn't say a word and Nell sat back and closed her eyes, determined to soak up every second of his company.

Having seen the last of the partygoers home, Ruth walked back up the hill, right to the top where rhododendrons flowered in a profusion of colour. She loved the soft light of evening, this quiet time of day when the cows ambled down towards the farmyard and lambs drew close to the ewes ready for the night.

The distant mountains looked black and shadowy now the sun had gone and there was a chill in the air which wouldn't go until morning.

She sat down on the damp grass and pulled the letter from her pocket. It was the second letter she'd received from Jimmy. The first had been quite a surprise, a pleasant one at that.

He wrote mostly about Eddie and didn't mention the war at all. That was his only reason for writing, she told herself firmly. It was no use letting herself think otherwise. They'd only met the one time and then only briefly. It would be foolish to read anything more into it than that.

That moment on the station, when it had felt to Ruth as though Jimmy had reached right inside her and touched her heart, could have been just a reaction to the poignancy of the situation.

She unfolded the sheet and her heart

began to beat faster when she recognised his untidy writing, yet when she'd finished the page, she felt disappointment settle around her.

What did she expect? His only concern was for Eddie and besides, a man like him was bound to have a woman waiting somewhere, probably in London.

'You've been spending a lot of time sitting up here on your own lately!'

She spun round, recognising Richard's accusing tones.

'Hello, Richard.' She found she was having to force a smile. At one time she would have welcomed his company, now she preferred her own. But he was so sensitive lately, that she had to tread on egg shells where his feelings were concerned.

'I thought you were helping Griff Thomas with a kids party?'

'I was, I did,' she said. 'It's all finished now. Eddie Walker's nan turned up, all the way from London.'

'So you came up here?'

'Anything wrong with that?' she snapped and could have bitten her tongue when she saw the expression of hurt cross his face.

'I know I'm not good company at the moment,' he said gloomily. 'I feel such a failure. I don't blame you for not wanting to spend more time with me.'

'It's not that, Richard,' she said sadly. 'I just wish you'd stop feeling so sorry for yourself, that's all.'

'It's not myself I feel sorry for,' he said vehemently. 'It's the boys in my class I know will be going to war before the end of the year! Kids I've taught, children who will be expected to become men. And my class next year ... They're playing games in the playground this year and next year they'll be given a gun and ordered to kill!'

She felt a surge of compassion for him and got to her feet so she could embrace him. He misunderstood the gesture and pulled her tightly to him, crushing her lips beneath his.

Struggling, she managed to get her hands up between them and push him away. He swayed slightly, putting the back of his hand against his mouth. Her own mouth felt bruised and her heart was pounding with fear. She'd never seen Richard like this before. Normally he was so gentle and considerate, he'd never dream of kissing her so roughly.

They stood for a moment, both shocked and bewildered, the darkness gathering around them, then as Ruth noticed something fluttering beside her feet, Richard grabbed for it.

'What's this?' he said.

'A letter,' she said, reaching to snatch it back. There was nothing in it he shouldn't read, but it incensed her that he should feel that he had the right.

'Who from?' he held it tantalisingly out of reach.

'A friend, let me have it back, Richard! It's nothing.'

'If it's nothing, you won't mind me reading it then.' He curled his lip.

'Don't be silly, it's getting dark. You

won't be able to read it anyway.'

'Silly, am I?'

He held the letter up in front of his face. There was still enough light left to read by and she watched his face go through a whole range of emotions, from anger, to pain and shock.

In the end, the hand holding the letter dropped at his side and he glared at her.

'From a soldier?' he said, his voice barely more than a whisper.

'Eddie's dad,' she said. 'He's not interested in me, just his son.'

'That's not how it reads to me,' he said. 'He seemed pretty interested in you if you ask me!'

'His interest in me is merely polite,' she said defensively, although why she should defend herself in this way was puzzling to her. She owed nothing to Richard, nothing at all. In fact, since she'd turned down his marriage proposal last December, they'd seen little of each other.

She had hoped whatever he felt for

her would die a natural death.

'I knew it would make you hate me,' he hissed. 'You're like all the rest! You don't think I'm a real man because I'm not over there fighting!'

'That's not fair, Richard!' she protested.

'But it's true! You'd prefer someone like this!' He waved the sheet of paper in her face. 'A real man!'

'No, Richard!'

'Then deny it!' he demanded furiously. 'Deny it. Tell me to my face that this ... this ... ' He consulted the paper. 'Jim Walker means nothing to you.'

Her silence went on for so long, that eventually he crumpled the letter in his fist and threw it to the ground before striding off down the hill into the darkness of the valley.

5

More bombers swept in from the west and Jimmy Walker was forced once again to dive for cover. How quickly things had changed when the order came to pull out. When they'd arrived at Dunkirk, there were already thousands there and smoke was spiralling up from the ruined town.

The chattering of machine-guns suddenly raked the air and Jimmy raised his head enough to see that they were picking out the most helpless, those halfway out to the boats.

'Come on.' He scrambled to his feet and pulled at the collar of the man beside him. 'We've got to get the wounded out.'

But the man did not respond for he was already dead. The beach was a mass of confusion, littered with bodies and no-one seemed to be in charge.

'Leave him.' Major David Anderson appeared beside him. 'We've no chance of getting on a boat for some time. If you want to help, we're getting the wounded back to Rosendale. I'd rather you got out of here — we never did find you a uniform!'

Jimmy, grateful for having something to do besides trying not to get killed, followed the major towards the beach. They worked well together as a team, pulling the wounded from the sea, getting them on to the trucks and ambulances bound for the British military hospital at the Chateau Rosendale.

Several times, they waded into the water to drag out the wounded as the sea bubbled all around them with machine-gun fire.

Sometimes when the trucks and ambulances broke down, Jimmy managed to get them going again so they could rattle up and down the road. He'd never seen so many men in all his life — or so much death. For the first time in his life, he understood, really understood, why his father's eyes had always been so haunted and sad.

Sights like this must live on in the memory for ever. So many young lives just thrown away, and what for..?

What had been a living nightmare became a battle for survival, not only his own, but that of his comrades. Night and day merged, the bombers all but ruined the roads to the hospital and the battle became a struggle. It was only when the wounded started to be sent back that Jimmy realised the futility of it all.

More than once during those nightmare days, his skill as a mechanic was called upon to keep the fleet of ambulances and trucks moving.

It was ironic when he'd spent the past few weeks doing as much damage as he could to enemy vehicles that he should now be using his mechanic's skill as a means of survival.

At least he'd managed to pass on the

information he'd gathered, so if anything did happen, if he should be killed here on this French beach, then his work of the past few weeks would not have been in vain.

He thought of his mother and smiled wrily. She had no idea what he'd been doing. Even before the war started, he'd been at work in Europe, yet she thought he was drifting aimlessly. Rather let her think that than know the truth and worry herself to death.

Right now she assumed he was a private in the army. It wasn't so far from the truth. Once they did get around to giving him a uniform, that's probably just what he'd be.

'All right, David?' he addressed the major. The young man was looking weary and bereft, confusion had set in, taking advantage of his exhaustion. His red-rimmed eyes turned to Jimmy.

'Just promise me one thing,' David murmured wearily. 'If I get hit, however badly, don't let them take me back to Rosendale. I'd rather take my chances on the boats . . . '

'Nothing's going to happen to you, David.' Jimmy laughed. 'We're charmed, you and me. We've proved that hundreds of times. If Jerry was going to get us, we'd have been gone by now.'

'I know.' David was solemn. 'Just promise me, Jim.'

'I promise,' Jimmy said.

Within a few hours, on the third of June, David was badly injured. Jimmy heard the burst of fire behind them and the pained cry and knew that David had been hit. It was as if he'd known it was almost his turn. He spun round, seeing the young man sprawled on the ground, blood seeping from his ragged uniform. Badly injured like that, he should go to the hospital, but after all they'd been through together over the past few days, Jimmy felt he owed him more than that.

He was unconscious and as limp as a rag doll as Jimmy dragged him into a semi-standing position. They'd done all they could, the pair of them; it was their turn now to get away. Tired, not having slept much, if at all over the past few days, Jimmy half carried, half dragged the major towards the water where few boats now waited.

Someone came and took half the weight and together they made it to the boats faster.

'He should be at the hospital,' an officer rapped.

'He's fine,' Jimmy lied and the officer let it pass. David was far from fine. He was very badly wounded and it was a long way back to England.

At last they got on the boat, a Thames barge already full of men. Several were German and Jimmy felt angered that they should be taking back prisoners of war when the places on the boats could have been put to better use.

'We'll soon be home, David,' he said, not knowing if he'd be able to hear or not. He was talking as much to reassure himself as his friend. Leaning back, he closed his eyes and thought of the nipper, safe on that farm in Wales.

'Thanks . . . Jimmy.'

He opened his eyes and realised David was conscious, eyes half open.

'Are you . . . '

'I'm OK,' David whispered.

The sound of more planes coming made them all silent. Surely they wouldn't fire on the boats, unarmed and defenceless as they were? If he lived to be a hundred, Jimmy knew he'd never forget the roar of the bombers, the sound of machine-gun fire and shells dropping. The screams of his fellow man would be ingrained for ever on his memory.

He felt the impact, rather than the pain when he was hit. Like something thumping into his head. Then a trickling in his hair. He raised his hand and it felt like lead. When he'd touched it to his head and felt the warm stickiness there, he pulled his hand back and looked at it, as if it didn't belong to him. Blood, thick and red, covered his fingers.

'I've been hit . . . ' he said to David, then everything went totally black.

'Will you go and fetch some water in, Eddie?' Griff asked and the little boy was eager to go. He'd be gone quite a while, Griff knew that. The little lad couldn't resist the animals and would probably stop to see them all on his way.

Nell looked across at him and smiled.

'You've really got a way with Eddie.' She smiled. 'You're a good man, Griff.'

He smiled and she wondered why his wife had ever gone off and left him. Over the past few days, she'd met quite a few people from the village and had learned about his wife leaving him.

'You never hear anything from your kids?' she said and his face at once darkened.

'Never,' he said.

'It's a shame,' she said. 'How old were they when . . . '

'Ten, eight and seven,' he said.

'Perhaps they'll come back,' she said.

'You know,' he said softly, 'I always

think of them as little children, but they're all of them grown up now. Old enough to go to war.'

'Why did she go, Griff?' Nell whispered. Her question wasn't asked from idle curiosity, but from concern.

'There was another man.' His eyes narrowed in pain. 'He came from Swansea, knew her before she married me. Everyone said I'd married above myself, and that it wouldn't last. She wasn't used to fetching her water in from outside or rising with the sun to see to the animals . . .

'But it wasn't just the water. She never felt at home here, never fitted in. I used to come in and find her crying . . . if he hadn't come, then someone else would.'

Nell shook her head. Perhaps Griff's wife would have settled in if she'd really wanted to, if she'd really loved him.

The door opened and Eddie came in, his chirpy face instantly lightening the atmosphere.

'You've been good to him, Griff,' Nell said. 'To both of us.'

'No.' Griff smiled. 'He's been good for me. And it's been good having you here, too, Nell.'

She smiled at him, revelling in the warmth of his golden eyes. These past few days spent with Eddie and Griff numbered among the happiest of her life, which was saying something in a country at war, with her only son in France.

Even before she came to Wales, she felt she knew the man. Being here, living in his house, watching him work, she had grown to more than like him. Beneath his gruff exterior was a truly gentle man. A gentle giant.

If it hadn't been for the war, she would never have met him and that thought made her feel very sad.

'I've been thinking, Griff,' she said. 'I really should be thinking about going home. I came for a day or two and I've been here two weeks . . . '

He looked shaken.

'But I thought . . . you seemed so happy here.'

'I have been, I am.' She reached over and touched his huge hand. 'Really. But I have a life in London and I should go back to it.'

'I understand.' He nodded, his golden eyes avoiding hers.

'No,' she said, smiling. 'I don't think you do. It's no reflection on your hospitality, Griff. I really meant it when I said I'd enjoyed my stay with you. We can still write . . . I can still come and visit.'

He looked up then and smiled.

'I hope so, Nell,' he said. 'Oh, I hope so.'

The railway station was busy, but not as packed as it had been. Even so, Nell realised she'd probably not get a seat, but it didn't bother her. She was well used to being on her feet.

'Why don't you stay?' Griff said. It was a last-ditch attempt on his part to get Nell to change her mind.

'I only ever intended to come for a

day, and I ended up staying a fortnight!' she said and ruffled her grandson's hair. 'I wanted to reassure myself that he was happy and . . . and I couldn't take care of him better myself, Griff.'

'There's room at the farm,' Griff said as the train chugged into the station. 'London's not going to be safe.'

'I've got to be there, in case there's news of my Jimmy,' she said. 'I want to know he got out of France and if he's all right. I know he'll let me know somehow.'

'You may hear nothing for a long time,' Griff warned.

'Give us a kiss.' She pulled Eddie into her arms and held him for a long time. For all she knew, it might be the last time she saw him. At least he wasn't as tearful as he'd been at their last parting, and that was some consolation at least.

Turning now to Griff, she reached up and kissed his rough cheek.

'Take care, now,' she said.

'*You* take care,' he said. 'We'll be all right.'

She stepped on to the train and Griff lifted Eddie up on to his shoulders so he could wave and not be lost in a sea of adults' legs.

A young sailor offered her his seat, but she shook her head.

'In a while perhaps,' she said. For all she wanted to do was stand up with her face touching the window, lost in her thoughts. It wasn't Eddie who troubled her, but her son. Eddie was fine, she'd seen that for herself, but as far as Jimmy was concerned, she didn't know if he was alive or dead.

She'd not let herself think about him at all during her time in Wales. Now she was on her way back to London and she could think of nothing else . . .

*   *   *

Mr Barker, head teacher at the village school, looked steadily at Ruth Lewis across his massive desk.

'I can't say I'm surprised, Ruth,' he said at last. 'Most people want to be part of the war effort and I can understand that. You feel that, tucked away here, you're not really a part of things. And you read such things in the newspapers . . . '

She said nothing, knowing there was more to come. She hadn't expected him to accept her resignation easily.

'But, Ruth, you must see that by being here, teaching the children — and there are so many here now — that you are doing something vitally important. These children are our hopes for the future, they are the future.'

'I know that, sir, but . . . '

'And there's Richard to consider. Have you thought of the effect this will have on him? It hit him hard you know, not being allowed to join up.'

Ruth looked away.

'Richard is not the issue here,' she said. 'We're friends, that's all . . . '

'Come now, Ruth, it's more than that and you do yourself a disservice to refer to your relationship as friendship. I've known Richard for some time and although he doesn't teach at this school, I admire him. You could do a lot worse than . . . '

'Forgive me, Mr Barker, but I've no intention of marrying Richard! There's a war on and frankly I'm fed up with reading about it and not being a part of it.'

'Foolish bravado, Ruth, foolish bravado. Do you think people enjoy being 'a part of things' as you put it?'

'I'm not interested in enjoyment, headmaster,' Ruth cried.

'So what do you intend to do? What skills can you offer?' His tone was derisory. 'Do you think, perhaps, that you could find work in an ordnance factory? Manufacturing instruments of death? Would you consider that a worthwhile occupation?'

'I don't know,' she said, flustered. 'I can drive, so perhaps I could drive ambulances or something.'

'Ambulances or something.' He repeated her words as if she were an errant seven year old pouring out feeble excuses for some misdemeanour. 'Try to be realistic, Ruth.'

'I am being realistic, sir! I don't think you realise how much this means to me!'

'And what will the school do without you? How shall we manage?'

'I've already thought of that,' she said. 'I've spoken to Miss Everson and she's more than willing to step in.'

'I still think you should talk it over with Richard before making a final decision,' Mr Barker said. 'Now if you'll excuse me . . . '

'Is that your final word on the subject?' Ruth said angrily. 'That you're not prepared to accept my resignation?'

'When you've spoken to Richard,' he reiterated, peering at her over the rim of his glasses, 'and given the matter some further thought, serious thought, then we shall discuss it further.'

She got up and stormed from the office, slamming the door behind her, not caring that the gesture was both futile and childish.

* * *

The pain in his skull was excruciating and when he tried to lift his head, it increased. Slowly he opened his eyes, knew at once he was in a hospital and found to his horror that that was all he knew.

He tried to think, but it caused pain just to do that. If only he could remember his name . . .

'Jimmy . . . '

There was nothing familiar about the voice or the name and no reason to think that anyone should be speaking to him, so he ignored it and continued to ignore it until the speaker actually clasped his shoulder and shook.

He looked up at the man standing beside his bed. His arm was swathed in bandages and his other arm gripped a crutch. His face, though pleasant, was unfamiliar.

'It's me, David,' the other man said.

'David?'

'Don't you remember? Dunkirk? The barge?'

'You called me Jimmy?'

'That's your name.'

'I'm thirsty . . . '

'Hold on, I'll get the nurse.'

The nurse duly came, gave him a drink and bustled about the bed, asking questions he found impossible to answer.

'Tell me . . . ' he implored David.

'Don't tire him,' the nurse said. 'It'll all come back in its own good time.'

David nodded and, using his crutch, limped towards Jimmy's bed and lowered himself carefully into a sitting position.

'You got a piece of shrapnel lodged in your head,' he said.

'Shrapnel?'

'At Dunkirk. Surely you remember something? You saved my skin for a start. I got it all down my left side, arm and leg.'

Jimmy forced himself to look up and saw that David's left leg was swathed in bandages.

90

'I could have lost it,' he said. 'It's battered and I'll probably end up with a limp for the rest of my life, but I'm not complaining!'

'What were we doing at Dunkirk?'

'The war.' David looked despairing. 'You really don't remember anything? Nothing at all? What about before the war? Where did you live?'

'I . . . I can't,' Jimmy cried out at last in desperation. The effort involved in trying to remember hurt too much and yet he wanted to remember, wanted to know who he was, where he came from.

'Do you want me to tell you what I know about you?' David suggested. 'I don't know much, but it may help trigger something.'

'Why . . . ?' Jimmy asked. 'Why should you want to do that?'

'Like I said, you saved my skin and besides, I like you.' David grinned. 'Now shall I tell you what I know — or what . . . ?'

★ ★ ★

91

'Before you go in, the doctor would like to have a word with you,' the nurse said kindly. Nell Walker's eyes widened. They were sad eyes, the nurse noted, full of worry and fear. She'd probably been told very little about her son's condition — if anything at all and was understandably anxious.

Identifying him had taken some time as he had arrived at the hospital looking for all the world like a European peasant with no identification on him whatsoever. It wasn't until the major was well enough to talk that any light was thrown on the situation at all.

'Will it take long?'

'He just wants to put you in the picture. Would you come this way?'

Nell sat down in a cool office, perched on the edge of her chair, handbag clasped on her knees. She hadn't seen so many hurt and injured young men since . . . since the last war and being here brought it all back.

'Sorry to keep you waiting.' The doctor who breezed in was in his early fifties, a competent-looking man. He had a folder in his hands and as he sat down, he opened it and looked at the papers inside.

'You're Jim Walker's mother?'

She nodded.

'What have you been told about his injuries?'

'Well, I phoned from the pub . . . They've been very kind, letting me use their phone.' She smiled nervously and realised she was waffling. 'I spoke to a nurse and she just said he was comfortable. And to be truthful, I don't much like telephones . . . I've always associated them with bad news . . . '

He watched her carefully. A busy man, he was obviously prepared to give her as much time as she needed.

'You'll be eager to see him,' he said.

'Oh, yes . . . '

'Before you do, there is something you should know.'

Nell straightened her shoulders and took in a deep breath. She'd come prepared for the worst and had told

93

herself that no matter how bad his injuries were, she'd let nothing show on her face.

She'd become an expert at hiding her feelings, and she only hoped she hadn't lost her old skills.

'I'm ready, doctor,' she said.

'The injuries to his body were very minor, easily treated. What has caused us the most concern are his head injuries. Two major ones were shrapnel actually embedded in his skull. The good news is that there are no indications of paralysis or notable loss of senses, except . . .

'Mrs Walker, I'm afraid that your son has suffered a memory loss. It's still too early to tell whether it is temporary . . . or not.'

'He won't know me?' Nell said resignedly.

'I very much doubt it.'

'Thank you, doctor.' She stood up. 'I'd like to see my son now.'

'Of course, follow me.'

He was sitting propped up in bed,

looking exactly the same except for the bandage wound around his head. Amnesia wasn't so bad, Nell told herself. A lot of mothers would have been glad to be in her shoes. The young man on the next bed was sitting on top of the covers, his left arm and left leg swathed in bandages.

'Hello,' the other man said. 'I'm David! You must be Jimmy's mum!'

Jimmy looked at her and for a moment she saw hope in his eyes, but it was soon replaced with emptiness. The doctor squeezed her shoulder lightly and left.

Nell approached the bed cautiously.

'Hello, Jim,' she said. 'How are you feeling?'

'Fine,' he said.

'He only woke up a couple of days ago, lazy begger.' David laughed, trying to ease the situation for Nell a little.

'I had a headache, but it's almost gone now,' Jimmy said.

'I've brought some things.' Blinded by tears she didn't want Jimmy to see,

Nell began to delve in her bag, pulling out brown paper parcels and putting them on the bed.

'Sit down,' Jimmy said.

Nell sank into a chair. She could hardly bring herself to look at him. He was like a stranger — or rather, she sensed that she was the stranger to him. He didn't know her from Adam and that hurt more than she ever thought possible.

'You . . . you do know who I am?' she asked.

'I assume you're my mother,' Jimmy replied. 'They told me you were coming. I'm sorry . . . I can't remember anything at all.'

The silence now was unbearable and Nell found herself wishing she hadn't come. With no memory there was nothing for them to talk about. She pulled herself up. Of course she could talk! Just pretend he did know, act normally, maybe that would help.

'I went to stay in Wales for a few days,' she said. 'I was there for Eddie's birthday. His seventh! You should see him. You'd never think he was the same scrawny little boy of last year! He's lost two of his front teeth and he's really caught the sun. He's so brown.

'He's staying with a nice man. Ruth Lewis was there and they had a party for him and everything . . .'

'Eddie?' Jimmy questioned.

'Your son.'

'I'm married?'

'Your wife died, don't you remember, Jim? Surely there must be something . . .'

He shook his head. 'I have a son.'

'Eddie, yes,' she said desperately. 'A grand boy.'

'A son.' Jimmy smiled and turned to look at David. 'Hear that, David? I have a son!'

'I heard.' David nodded.

'Tell me about him . . . what do I call you? Ma? Mum? Mother?'

'Mum, usually.' Nell smiled. 'But a few other things if you're annoyed!'

They all laughed.

'I can't imagine being annoyed with you,' Jimmy said and she saw some of the old tenderness back in his eyes. 'Do I have a dad?'

'He died,' she said. 'There's just been you and me and little Eddie.'

'And he's in Wales?'

'On a farm.' She nodded.

He grinned. 'All right, Mum,' he said. 'Tell me about Eddie. I want to know everything about him. Is he like me?'

'Poor little devil!' David exploded with laughter from the next bed. 'Don't wish that on him!'

6

'I'll stay until the summer holidays,' Ruth said. 'What do you think?'

'Does it really matter what I think?' Richard said resignedly. 'You'll go, whatever I say.'

'Yes, Richard, I will. But I promised Mr Baker I'd talk it over with you first.'

'And that's the only reason you wanted to talk to me? Because you promised him?'

'Because I didn't want you hearing it from someone else. We've been close, Richard. I don't want to jeopardise our friendship.'

'I know we haven't exacty been seeing eye to eye lately, Ruth, but — '

'I won't change my mind, Richard!' She got up and moved away from him and stood on the hillside looking out across the valley.

Silently, he came up behind her and

placed his hands gently on her shoulders.

'Whatever you decide to do, Ruth, I'll be proud of you.'

Slowly, she turned round to look at him and could see at once that he meant every word.

'I know I've been bitter and I've behaved stupidly, but I think I'm over that, now. Go, Ruth, go with my blessing. It's time we both started afresh.'

She touched his mouth with her lips, but the kiss, although tender, was without passion.

'What will you do?' he asked.

'I'm going to London,' she said. 'And I'll take it from there.'

'Well, I wish you luck, Ruth. Come and say goodbye to me before you leave. It won't be long now, will it?'

'As soon as . . . '

'Miss Lewis, Miss Lewis . . . '

Ruth jerked her head round and saw a child from the school scrambling up the hill towards them.

'It's Mrs Ellis . . . ' the child rasped breathlessly. 'She's had another bad turn, miss . . . '

As soon as she received the news about her landlady, Ruth broke into a run. She knew Mrs Ellis was frail and often had bad turns. This time, it was far more serious than usual. Mrs Ellis had suffered a heart attack.

'It looks as though I'll have to shelve my plans to go to London, at least for a while,' Ruth told Richard in hushed tones. 'She's going to need me . . . '

Ruth stayed until the September of 1940 when she left for London.

The summer was a long one for Nell Walker. She made frequent trips to the hospital, but one visit which stuck in her mind more than any others was the one when Jimmy had looked up at her and asked, 'Did we have a cat once called Sammy?'

She almost choked.

'Tabby,' he went on. 'Green eyes, used to catch rats and bring them home then lay them at your feet . . . ?'

'Sammy,' she whispered, sinking into the chair. 'We got him when you were still small. Beautiful cat he was and, oh, how you loved him! You must have been fifteen when he died and you were heartbroken ... Oh, Jimmy, do you really remember him?'

'I can remember something else, Mum,' he said. 'My dad, carrying me down to the docks on his shoulders. I thought I was the tallest person in the world ... and football, on a Saturday afternoon ... '

After that, it was ten long days before anything else came back and that's how the summer went. Memory returning in dribs and drabs and sometimes in chunks, but however it was happening, Nell knew she was getting her son back.

He even started talking about the future, about what he'd do after the war. He and David together, talking about the garage.

'The war's over for David now, Mum,' he told her on one visit. 'All our lads from the garage have gone to fight, so why don't we let him take it over for us?'

'I could keep it ticking over . . . ' David said eagerly.

'I think that's a marvellous idea,' Nell agreed. 'But what about you, Jim? You won't be fighting, will you?'

He hadn't answered her question. He didn't know how to.

It was only when Nell was sure he was going to be all right that she wrote to Griff and told him what had happened, asking him to explain things to Eddie.

Then came the greatest shock of all, arriving at the hospital to find someone else in Jimmy's bed and Jimmy wearing a uniform.

'They can't send you back!' Nell's self-control vanished. 'Not after all you've been through! You're not fit!'

'I know I'm not fit.' He grinned. 'But I'll get fit. This war's not over yet and I want another chance.'

'After what happened to you? Are you mad?'

'We're going to win this war, Mum. One way or another. Don't look so worried, darlin'. I'll be staying over here until I'm properly fit.'

He hugged her.

'Then what?' She went stiff in his arms, rigid with fear. 'When you're fit, they'll send you overseas! I don't want to lose you, Jim.'

'You won't lose him, Mrs Walker!' David called out. 'We've been trying to lose him for weeks and it's impossible, I'll tell you!'

Despite herself, she laughed, David's cheery banter had worked again.

Jimmy tilted her chin.

'That's right, Mum, you have a good laugh! I'll be all right. There's nothing going to stop me coming back to you and Eddie, nothing, I promise you that . . .'

'What are you doing here?' Nell cried upon seeing Ruth Lewis standing at her door. 'Is it Eddie? What's happened?'

She half expected to see her grandson's cheeky face appear round the corner, but Ruth was quite alone.

'Eddie's fine.' Ruth smiled. 'Can I come in? I've one or two things here . . . '

'Of course.' Nell's face broke into a smile. 'It's good to see you, Ruth. But what on earth are you doing in London? They bombed the Surrey Docks a few days ago.'

'I heard,' Ruth said. 'I've come to do my bit,' she explained with a cheerful grin. 'I'm going to drive an ambulance.'

'An ambulance?' Nell gasped. 'But what about the school?'

'A retired mistress is standing in for me,' Ruth said.

'I'll make you a cup of tea,' Nell said. 'Sit down.'

Ruth sat at the small table while Nell bustled about setting out cups.

'I've no sugar, I'm afraid,' Nell said apologetically. 'I used the last of it this morning to make Jimmy a cake.'

At last she sat down and Ruth began to unpack her bag on to the table.

'Eggs — from Griff,' she said. 'Some

bacon, a chicken ... ' She smiled, seeing Nell's delight. 'A letter from Griff and one from Eddie and this ... from all of us.'

She set a photograph on the table. It was Eddie, laughing cheekily at the camera, his new teeth already growing strongly. Tears gathered in Nell's eyes and she quickly dabbed at them with her handkerchief.

She picked the photograph up and studied it closely.

'I don't know what to say,' she said. 'How is he? How is Griff?'

'They're both fine. Griff wants you to go to Wales, especially since this bombing started.'

'This is my home,' Nell said stubbornly. 'We moved in here when Jimmy was just a small boy. It's the first place I ever lived that didn't belong to someone else.'

'I knew you'd say that.' Ruth grinned. 'Griff told me about Jimmy.' Her expression became sober. 'How is he?'

'He remembers some things.' Nell shrugged. 'Things I'd rather he forgot.'

'Such as?'

'Such as his determination to fight! I feel that we're so alone, Ruth, so alone! Our one nation standing up to Hitler's might and now it seems he's turned all that fury on us. Jimmy's determined to go back.'

'Where is he now?'

'Light duties.' Nell shrugged. 'Until he's fit enough for action. How about you? Are you fixed up with somewhere to stay yet?'

'I only arrived this morning.' Ruth smiled. 'I suppose I'll be spending most of my time at the ambulance station.'

'If they let you have any time off,' Nell said. 'You're welcome to stay with me. There's Eddie's room.'

'Thanks,' Ruth said. 'I'll take you up on that! I want to visit my cousin's house ... well ... my house now, sometime, too. But it won't be fit to live in, it's been empty for years. I've neglected it terribly.'

'Do you mind . . . ?' Nell held up the letters.

'Go ahead,' Ruth said. 'I'll pour the tea, shall I?'

It didn't take long to read the one page from Eddie. In a way, Nell was glad that he didn't have time to write more. Long letters usually came from lonely and unhappy children.

Griff had written pages. Strange, he was such a silent man, yet so clever at expressing himself on paper. He begged her to go back to Wales, yet at the same time understood her reasons for staying where she was.

Her vision failed her and she went to a drawer for her spectacles. Ruth remained silent looking around at her surroundings. This neat, little house was certainly unlike Eddie's home on the farm.

Nell obviously took great pride in her home. Everywhere was clean and freshly polished, yet there was a ragged old picture on the wall, drawn by Eddie. It was curling at the edges and must have been hanging up there for over a year.

She heard footsteps on the pathway outside and expected them to go on past, but instead, they stopped and the door opened.

Jumping to her feet, Ruth found herself facing Jimmy and all those strange, confusing feelings rushed back, stronger than ever. She wondered then how much of her desire to come to London had been for this reason, to see him and not for the reasons she'd given herself and everyone else.

He looked just the same, a little more handsome in uniform, but the eyes still sparkled, the cheeks still dimpled when he grinned.

'Wait,' Nell said before anyone could speak. 'I've told him a little about you. Jimmy, do you remember who this is?'

He stared at her for a moment and Ruth held her breath, her heart pounding behind her ribs. Suddenly it was vitally important that he should know her.

'Ruth,' he said at last. 'You're Ruth.'

★ ★ ★

She held his arm as they walked through the streets and he stopped before a road which had been barricaded off. Where once houses had stood, now were piles of rubble and masonry.

'I wish you hadn't come here.' Jimmy spoke for the first time since they'd left the house. 'You'd have been safer in Wales.'

'I wanted to come, Jim,' she said softly.

'It's still sketchy — my memory,' he said. 'Were we . . . I mean, I don't want to put my foot in it.'

She tugged on his arm and they moved away from the bombed street. Now was her chance to be honest about her feelings. He couldn't have made it any easier for her, yet there was no way of putting her feelings into words.

Besides, with his amnesia, it would have been like taking advantage.

'We only met once,' she said at last. 'When you came to see Eddie just after he'd been evacuated.'

'Oh.' He sounded disappointed. 'It's just that, when I saw you in Mum's kitchen, I . . . It was as if you really meant something to me.'

He stopped walking and turned to look at her. Ruth's heart seemed to flip right over.

'Does that sound stupid to you? I'm sorry,' he rushed on. 'You've probably got someone, I've no right . . . '

'There's no-one,' she said, thinking guiltily of Richard despite the fact that he'd at last let her go.

'I ought to be getting back to the ambulance station,' she said, aware of the time.

'Ruth . . . wait.'

She stopped in her tracks and turned to look at him.

'Will I see you again?' he asked.

'Yes.' She smiled. 'You will, Jimmy. I promise.'

She didn't go straight to the ambulance station, but took the bus to the part of London where she'd grown from a child to a young woman.

Cousin Rachel's house looked no different to the first time she'd seen it, except perhaps the ivy had scrambled where it shouldn't, obliterating some of the windows.

She stepped up to the front door, having to make her way through an undergrowth of nettles and thistles, and felt a sudden surge of shame for allowing the house to fall into such a state.

It was rather gothic in style, a tall, looming house with a turret at one corner upon which stood a pointed roof like a witch's hat. She fumbled for her key, twisted it in the stiff lock and let herself into the dark hallway.

A thick covering of dust lay everywhere and Ruth's shame deepened.

'I'm sorry, Rachel,' she whispered

into the musty emptiness. 'I'm so sorry.'

Then she left quickly, without looking farther into the house, promising herself to return at a later date when she could make a start on getting the house in order.

★ ★ ★

Nell finished reading the letter at last and with a sigh, laid it down on the table top. She'd been quite pleased when Jimmy suggested taking Ruth for a walk and was doubly so now she'd read Griff's final paragraph.

A slow smile formed on her mouth and she laughed out loud. Griff's marriage proposal had come as a complete surprise, yet ... it wasn't totally unexpected.

He hadn't actually mentioned love, but he reckoned his life had found new meaning since he met her. She was unique, he said, unlike anyone he'd ever known before.

'I'd like nothing more than to be

Eddie's Grandad,' he'd written and now, as Nell read aloud the final paragraph, she couldn't help smiling at his strange choice of words.

'If you think these words are just the insane ramblings of a simple farmer, then cut this bit out of the letter and throw it away and I beg you to forget it was ever written, for I value our friendship more than anything else. But I can think of nothing but marrying you, Nell.'

The letter then finished abruptly.

She jumped when the door closed and turned to see Jimmy standing there alone.

'Where's Ruth?'

'She had to report to the ambulance station,' he said. 'Mum, she says we only met once, yet I feel as though . . . as though she meant something to me.'

Nell smiled and nodded. 'Perhaps she did, son,' she said. 'She's a very nice girl. I'm not surprised she made an impact!'

7

What began as a quiet night was plunged into noise and mayhem, heralded by the wailing of the air-raid sirens. Ruth hadn't been able to sleep anyway. She'd sat drinking tea and chatting to the other girls on her shift.

'Know your districts, do you?' Jean, one of the other drivers, asked.

'I should do,' Ruth said. 'I've been studying the maps for weeks and it's little changed since I lived here.'

The other ambulance drivers exchanged looks.

'I know what you must think,' Ruth said softly. 'But I really — '

They heard the bombers droning overhead and Ruth shuddered. She hadn't expected the noise to be so loud — or so terrifying. She jumped visibly as the anti-aircraft guns started up.

Then the bombs started to drop so

that the ground shook. Where incendiaries hit, the night sky was lit with crimson flames.

Ruth had never been so frightened in all her life. After all she'd read, all she'd heard and come to expect, the reality was much, much worse. She began to wish, earnestly wish with all her heart, that she hadn't come, that she'd stayed in the safety of the valley.

'Stirrup pump!' someone yelled and Ruth rushed outside to find small fires crackling and spitting in the street outside the ambulance station.

She set to with the pump and at first, it seemed the more they tried to put the little fires out, the more determinedly they burned. She looked up, saw the sky criss-crossed with light, the flames of a blazing plane streaking down . . .

'One of them?' she asked.

'Oh, yes,' Jean said. 'You can be sure of that!'

'Come on, Ruth! Your first call!'

She rushed back into the station and before she had time to think, was racing through the streets in the ambulance, her attendant beside her yelling directions. The skyline was aglow with burning buildings and as she drove, the bombs seemed to be falling all around her.

Already the rescue effort had begun.

It seemed to Ruth that night, that London, the part she was in anyway, had been completely destroyed. She lost count of the number of times she was called out, the amount of injured people she ferried to the hospital.

Even after the 'All Clear' was sounded, she was still kept busy until the day shift arrived to take over.

'Baptism of fire, Ruthie!' Jean squeezed her shoulder. 'How do you feel?'

'Sick,' Ruth replied truthfully.

'You probably will be. It was a bad night — the worst yet for us. Is there anywhere you can go?'

Ruth nodded.

'Off you go then, love. See you tonight, God willing.'

Nell's mouth widened in shock when she saw Ruth. The girl's pale face was streaked with dirt, her dark hair white with dust and her weary, red eyes filled with horror.

'Now perhaps you'll see sense and go back to Wales,' Nell said sternly as she put water on to heat for Ruth to wash. 'This is no place for a young woman, especially if she doesn't need to be here.

'I'll make you a cup of tea and something to eat, then you can get your head down. I daresay you'll be back in the thick of it again tonight.

'There's a house out the back there completely gone! The family was in the shelter, thank goodness! I've got that bacon here that Griff sent. How do you like it? My Jim likes it crisp and . . . Ruth?'

Ruth was slumped over the table, her head resting on her arms, sound asleep.

Nell tried to gently wake her, but

Ruth was off sound, so she fetched a blanket and draped it around the girl's shoulders.

'If you're like this after one night — ' Nell shook her head. 'How are you going to be after a week of it? You'll never cope with it, girl. It'll kill you!'

When Jimmy got in an hour later, Ruth was in the same position at the table, still sleeping. Nell put her finger to her lips when he walked in.

'How long's she been there?' he asked.

'An hour. I couldn't wake her so I thought I'd best leave her.'

'She can't sleep like that!' Jimmy said. 'She'll wake up all stiff and if she has another night of it tonight, she's going to need all the rest she can get.'

'I told you, I can't wake her,' Nell said indignantly.

'Then I'll put her to bed myself,' he retorted. 'Open the door, Mum, and turn back the sheets on Eddie's bed for her.'

Carefully, he moved the blanket from

Ruth's shoulders and manoeuvred her into his arms. She barely stirred, murmured something and smacked her lips, like a child enjoying a dream.

He was surprised at how little she weighed, how slight and small her body felt in his arms. Quickly, he carried her through to Eddie's room and laid her in the bed. Nell was waiting to cover her over and they closed the curtains, then the door, leaving her to sleep on.

'If you're going to be here for dinner,' Nell said once they were in the kitchen, 'I'll cook that chicken. And by the way, I suppose you should know, Griff Thomas has asked me to marry him.'

Jimmy sat down at the table with the paper, flicked it open and began to read.

'Chicken sounds great, Mum,' he said, then he stopped and looked up at her. 'What did you say about Griff Thomas?'

'He wants to marry me,' she said, her cheeks flushing pink.

'Why?'

'What do you mean, why?' Nell cried.

'I'm sorry, Mum.' He rubbed his hand across his face. 'I must have got things wrong somewhere along the line. I didn't realise you knew him that well.'

'I didn't . . . don't. But he's been good to our Eddie and he's a kind and gentle man . . .'

'That's no reason to marry someone,' he said. 'Do you love him?'

She looked away.

'I think I could,' she said at last. 'Given time.'

'More to the point, does he love you?' Jimmy went on bluntly. 'Or does he want a woman to take care of him in his old age?'

Nell's cheeks flamed with colour.

'How dare you? If you weren't still convalescing, I'd hit you for saying that!'

He went to her, put his hands on her shoulders and kissed her forehead. Her skin burned beneath his lips. He hadn't meant to insult her or hurt her feelings.

'Let's not fall out, Mum, not now.'

She forgave him and got on with the lunch. When it came to carving the chicken, Nell distributed it between several plates.

'I'll give some to the Collins and a bit of meat to Carrie from number five. She needs it now she's nursing that baby. There's enough for old Mr Deeks to have some, too — '

'Save some for yourself for tomorrow,' Jimmy said. 'You can have it cold.'

'I may not be here tomorrow, Jim,' she said. 'We might all have gone up in smoke by then.'

'Live for today, eh?' Jimmy grinned, then Ruth walked in, feeling refreshed after her sleep.

'I don't even remember walking here,' she said. 'Let alone going to bed!'

'Perhaps now you'll see sense,' Nell said. 'And go back to Wales where you belong.'

'Last night was awful,' Ruth said. 'But I did some good. For the first time in my life I feel useful, needed, like I was doing something worthwhile.'

'I bet you're hungry,' Jimmy said. 'Sit down, we're eating Griff's chicken!'

'Eddie's chicken.' Ruth smiled ruefully as she took a seat at the table. 'He called her Nellie, after his nan.'

'Oh!' Nell looked at the meat piled on her plate.

'Don't worry about it.' Ruth smiled. 'Griff gave him a new hen and he's called her Mr Churchill, so next time he sends you a chicken, you could tell people you'd had Mr Churchill for lunch!'

They all laughed and Nell's appetite returned as quickly as it had vanished.

When lunch was over, the remains of the chicken divided between Nell's closest neighbours and the washing-up done, Nell sat down in her armchair and took up her knitting. Within minutes, she was sound asleep.

'Shall we go for a walk?' Jimmy suggested. 'Or are you going to get your head down for a few hours before you go to work?'

'A walk sounds lovely,' she said and

once again, it came quite naturally to her to hold his arm. This time, Jimmy took her by a route which by-passed the new bomb sites. She didn't need reminding of the night before.

In the park, in the sun, there was little to remind them of the war, apart from the presence of so many uniforms. Last night seemed a hundred years ago, yet the smell of smoke still hung in the air and fires still burned all over the capital.

They sat down together on the grass and talked. Conversation came easily to them. Any silences were comfortable and their laughter was real. Ruth had never felt like that before, not with anyone, not even with Richard who, at one time, had meant more to her than anyone else ever had.

Jimmy talked a lot about what he was going to do after the war. He planned to go into business with a friend called David. David's war was over and he was eager to plan for the future.

'I want to build the business my

father started into something big,' Jimmy said. 'Something solid and real for my kids to inherit in years to come.'

'Kids?' Ruth laughed.

'Oh, yes! There's Eddie, of course, but I like kids. There's still time for me to marry again, start a family.'

'Is that what you want?'

He shrugged. 'I'd never thought about it until today — at least, I don't think I had. Did you know Griff Thomas had proposed to my mother?'

'I guessed he would,' Ruth said. 'He's been a recluse since his wife left him, shutting everyone out of his life. Eddie changed all that and Griff's a different man now. People who knew him years ago say he's back to his old self.'

'I wish he hadn't asked her now,' Jimmy said, looking up at the sun and squinting.

'Why not?'

'Because we're at war and emotions get mixed and muddled up and no-one can be sure of anything. People rush into marriage and maybe they'll live to regret it because one day, next year, in five years or however long it takes, this war will be over and they'll have to live with each other.'

'But if they're in love . . . ' Ruth began.

He turned to look at her, scorching her with his eyes.

'People change. How can a man kill other men, see his friends butchered, have to do things no human being should ever have to do, and not be changed?

'My father used to curl up and cry whenever there was a thunderstorm. He used to weep and sob like a baby because the noise brought the hell of the trenches back to him all over again.'

'But Nell still loved him,' she said softly.

'Yes, yes she did,' he said. 'But what kind of a life was it for her? The man she married was killed in France along with thousands of his comrades. Only his shell came back.'

'I don't want to hear you talking like

this,' Ruth said. 'Things are different now. You've already survived Dunkirk.'

'How about you?' he said. 'How long do you think you can go on patching people up and driving them to hospital? How long before it gets to you?'

'I'll do it for as long as I have to,' she said.

'Let's not argue about it any more.' He smiled and his face was at once transformed.

He reached out and touched her face, stroking her smooth skin with his fingers. She shivered at his touch and as he made to draw his hand away, she covered it with her own and held it against her face.

For a long time, they stayed exactly in that position, staring at each other, both longing for the next move, each afraid to make it. At last it was Jimmy who slowly pulled her face to his until their lips were inches apart.

At last their lips met, tentatively at first, then Jimmy was holding her in his arms, crushing her within his embrace.

There was something fierce and possessive about the way he kissed her, yet he didn't hurt or frighten her the way Richard had.

She responded, holding him close, not caring who might see. Emotions were laid bare everywhere she looked and no-one found the passionate embraces of lovers embarrassing or distasteful.

'Tell me now, Ruth,' he breathed when at last they parted. 'Tell me there wasn't something between us before! Because when I kiss you, I feel as though I'm coming back somewhere I always longed to be.'

'There was nothing,' she said at last. 'Attraction perhaps, but we really did only meet once.'

'But I feel . . . ' He broke off. 'I'm sorry.'

'Don't be sorry.' She touched his face and made him look into her eyes. 'I'm not sorry.'

He got to his feet.

'Where are you going?' she said.

'Jimmy, what's wrong?'

'Everything,' he said. 'You and me, everything!'

She scrambled to her feet and grabbed his arm.

Was this how Richard felt when she rejected him? Had she inflicted this amount of pain on him?

'I love you, Jimmy!' she said, gripping his arm.

'No, you don't, can't you see?' he pleaded with her. 'I could be sent away at any time. If I didn't wear this uniform . . . '

'You weren't wearing a uniform the first time we met,' she said.

'Oh, Ruth, try to understand . . . '

He looked at her, but she couldn't read the expression in his eyes. She did love him, she knew it as sure as she knew anything and it wasn't just the uniform or the war, it was him.

'Is there someone else?' she said. 'Is that what you're trying to tell me?'

He laughed then. 'No, there's no-one else. There's been no-one since my wife died. We married at eighteen, had to, did my mother tell you that?'

Ruth shook her head.

'Did you love her very much?' she said.

'As much as I could,' he murmured. 'We were just kids, both of us, stupid kids. I thought she was the love of my life, I really did, until . . . '

'Until when, Jimmy?'

He shrugged. 'We'd better be getting back. Mum will wonder where we are.'

'Jimmy.' She took hold of his hand and when he turned to look at her, she saw the pain in his eyes. Pain she'd dredged up without meaning to.

'I meant what I said,' she said. 'I'm sorry, but I can't change the way I feel.'

'If I said I loved you, too, what difference would it make?' he said. 'I couldn't ask you to wait for me, Ruth. I wouldn't do that. I can't offer you anything.'

'All I'm asking for is your love,' Ruth said, blinded by tears. 'Don't humiliate me like this, Jimmy!'

'Humiliate you?' he whispered, pulling her into his arms. 'Humiliate you? How could I ever do that, Ruth? You mean too much to me. Can't you see, that's why I won't make any promises. All right, I'll tell you the truth. I do love you. Seeing you in Mum's house yesterday, I felt as if someone had thumped all the air out of me.

'I knew then that I loved you and it felt as though I'd loved you for ever. I half hoped that someone would tell me that you were my wife, or fiancée or someone special they'd been keeping secret.

'But I've been through it all once, Ruth. I ruined Rose's life. She died after having Eddie, so it was my fault. I don't want to wreck your life, too.'

He held her to him, kissed her passionately, then pushed her away.

'I love you, Ruth, but don't wait for me! If you meet someone else before I come back, I'll understand, but don't waste your life waiting for someone you may never see again.

'I have every intention of coming home, but so has every other man. Do you understand what I'm saying, Ruth?'

She nodded, too choked to speak. It didn't matter what he said, she intended to wait, even if it took the rest of her life.

He took her hand in his, squeezed it and grinned.

'Let's go home. Mum will want you to have something hot to eat before you go on duty.'

She nodded and walked along beside him.

8

Miles away, in the Welsh valley, Griff Thomas tried to calm the boy. He was like a cat with a fish bone stuck in its throat, pacing the floor, howling with pain, eyes wild and terrified.

'Me nan,' he said, clutching at Griff's shirt. 'You don't understand, it's me nan!'

The news from London had been getting steadily worse and Eddie was bright enough to pick it all up.

'They've got bomb shelters, Eddie,' Griff said unconvincingly, wishing he knew how to put the boy's mind at rest once and for all.

'But what if she don't make it?' Eddie said. 'What if one of them bombs drops on her?'

'She'll be all right,' Griff said, gritting his teeth. 'She's not daft . . .'

The next morning, Griff knew by the

heartbroken weeping coming from Eddie's room that the boy had wet the bed again. It was the first time since the early days.

Silently, he picked the boy up and rocked him in his arms until the sobs subsided.

'I'll tell you what,' Griff said at last, desperate to placate the child. 'I'll take you to London myself and you can see for yourself that she's alive and well!'

'Home?' Eddie's tear-stained face was suddenly joyful. 'I'm going home?'

'The land girls will have to take care of the farm,' Griff said, a little regretfully. 'And we can take her some of Mr Churchill's eggs!'

Eddie's face was wreathed in smiles as he wriggled down. The misgivings Griff had felt at first for suggesting such a reckless thing, were quickly banished.

He'd like to see Nell, too, see that she was safe and maybe persuade her to come back to Wales.

Yes, he decided. The autumn of 1940

was a good time for him to take Eddie to London.

*   *   *

'I don't think I can stand another night down the tube shelter,' Nell said. 'I never did care much for crowds of people and sometimes the stench is more than I can bear.'

Ruth looked up from her breakfast. She'd just completed a whole week as an ambulance driver and was adapting to things much better now. She'd got into a pattern of sleeping and eating which fitted in with her night shifts.

Nell was gazing into space thoughtfully.

'Where else would you go?' Ruth said.

Nell shrugged. 'Take my chances here, I suppose. Not everyone goes underground.'

'Not everyone survives the raids,' Ruth reminded her. 'I know, I have to pick up the pieces, remember?'

'I'll wash these up.' Nell got up abruptly and gathered the dishes together. 'You go and get some sleep. I'll wake you at two.'

'I'll give you a hand,' Ruth said.

'Did Jimmy tell you that he might not get home today?' Nell blurted out suddenly. 'Only I haven't seen him since breakfast yesterday and I'm worried.'

'He's a soldier, Nell,' Ruth said softly. 'He has to go where they tell him. You've been lucky to see as much of him as you have.'

'Lucky?' Nell's voice shook. 'Lucky? I almost lost him.'

'But you didn't,' Ruth said, putting her arms around Nell's shoulders. 'He's still very much alive.'

'Oh, you're right.' Nell sighed. 'I'm just a silly, old woman. Go on to bed, Ruth, get your sleep. He'll turn up sooner or later . . . probably when he's hungry! That was always his way!'

In Eddie's room, Ruth sat on the bed, deep in thought. There was a small stack of comics in one corner of the room and a little, wooden crane. She picked it up and looked at it, imagining the little boy winding the handle, picking up the neat little bundles with the hook.

She could no longer understand Nell's determination to remain in London. Each night was a nightmare, worse than the night before. Yet something miraculous had happened to the people. The more bombs the Germans dropped on them, the more determined they became to dig their heels in and fight.

Very few were fleeing the city. People stayed, picking over the wreckage of their homes, finding refuge with friends, neighbours, strangers . . .

People who normally didn't speak were suddenly comrades.

There was little detail in the newspapers about the destruction and Ruth was glad of that. Eddie was a good reader and liked to read the papers. She hated to think of him being frightened by events in his home.

Hearing the drone of a plane, she rushed to the window to look out.

'No,' she whispered seeing the black bombs falling. Then came the explosions that shook the ground.

'No,' Nell said, rushing into the room and pulling the curtains. 'You should be in bed. What happens during the day isn't your concern. You need your strength for the nights, Ruth.'

'I just wish . . . '

'I know, Ruth.' Nell put her arms around her. 'I know. We all do. But it can't go on for ever. It's got to stop sometime.'

Eddie fidgeted in his seat. The train was half empty and he'd lost interest in the scenery rushing by the window. A year had passed since he left his home in London, a whole year. He could hardly remember what it was like before he lived in Wales.

He couldn't imagine getting water straight from the tap again, or walking to the sounds of traffic and trains and people instead of the lowing of cattle and the barking of dogs.

He remembered the journey to Wales though. The crowded train, the dirt, the noise of children crying. He'd thought it would never end and when it did, there had been the awful fear, the knowledge that he was all alone in a strange land.

If it hadn't been for Miss Lewis's kindness . . .

'Feel all right, do you?' Griff asked. 'Want a sandwich?'

'Not hungry,' Eddie said. 'Do you think Nan's all right?'

'Of course she is,' Griff said. 'Things aren't so bad in London.'

'Do you think we'll see Miss Lewis?'

Griff didn't answer, too lost in thought to hear Eddie's question.

'Uncle Griff . . . ' Eddie prodded his arm. 'Do you think we'll see Miss Lewis? She's in London, isn't she? Do you think she'll have been to see Nan? Do you reckon she's seen my dad? Will my dad be there?'

Griff smiled at the boy.

'We'll find out in a few hours,' he said, wearied by Eddie's constant barrage of unanswerable questions. 'I'm going to have a nap now, Eddie.'

He closed his eyes and heard Eddie's exasperated sigh.

'Soon be there,' he said sleepily, keeping his eyes shut.

★　★　★

Ruth had just sat down in the duty room when the air-raid siren went.

It wouldn't be long now before the first wave of bombers came over, then the ambulances would be called out. For Ruth, the waiting was the worst part. It played havoc with her nerves. She felt much better once she was actually doing something.

Some of the other girls were playing cards, but Ruth couldn't concentrate on the game. She kept thinking of Nell, hoping she'd had the sense to go down to the shelter.

While Ruth waited for her first call out, Nell sat at her kitchen table, drumming her fingers on the top. Maybe she was daft not to go down to the shelter, but she just couldn't face it tonight. Tomorrow maybe, the next day, but not tonight.

One of the neighbours knocked on her door.

'You there, Nell?' she called out. 'We're off down the tube . . . Are you coming?'

Nell remained silent, holding her breath.

'She must have gone,' she heard the neighbour call to her husband. Then they were gone and everywhere was completely still and silent.

Ruth would be cross — Jimmy would be mad if he knew, but Nell was tired and wanted to sleep in her own bed for a change.

She got up and felt her way through the darkness to her bedroom. At least she knew Eddie was safe, at least there was that. Right now, he'd be tucked up in bed in that cosy Welsh farmhouse.

She smiled at the thought of Griff, sitting in that big, old, fireside chair. One of his old collies would probably have its head on his feet. Yes, she thought, she'd like to be there in that peaceful valley, but not yet. Not until this was all over and she could say she left London because she wanted to, not because she was chased out.

Maybe that was it, she decided, slipping down beneath the sheets. She wasn't prepared to leave London until she could do it of her own accord, because she wanted to. She wanted no-one to be able to say that she was hounded out of her own home, that she left through fear.

When Nell Walker left London, it would be because she wanted to and she wasn't about to leave it in ruins!

* * *

Some distance away, the big Welshman stood holding the little boy's hand, looking all around him in confusion. When the air-raid siren went off, the people around him took off in all directions, all of them appearing to know exactly what to do and where to go.

Griff had still been reeling from the shock. He'd never have brought Eddie here if he'd known what awaited them. They'd walked the streets in silence, viewing the bomb damage and the fires with disbelief. They'd seen people pushing all they had in the world on hand carts, others tearing at the rubble with their bare hands.

There was a bus service operating, but Griff was completely lost and Eddie seemed too shocked to know which way to go.

'Come this way.' A woman grasped Griff's arm. 'The basement . . . you'll be safe there.'

Thankfully, Griff followed the woman.

'What about Nan?' Eddie said.

'We'll find her tomorrow,' Griff said. 'I promise.'

There was quite an atmosphere in the basement. The house belonged to a wealthy family, but provided shelter for people from all backgrounds. The lady who had found them lost in the street brought them each a blanket and smiled reassuringly at Eddie.

'I'm Mrs March,' she said. 'My husband, the doctor, is out tonight — as every night. Would you like anything to eat?'

'No, thank you,' Griff said and carefully wrapped one of the blankets he'd been given around Eddie.

'Is this your first night in London?'

Griff nodded.

'It will get very noisy,' she said. 'But try not to be frightened. We're very safe down here. What made you come to London?'

As they spoke, the first of the bombers came. Eddie sat bolt upright as the anti-aircraft guns went into action.

'I wish I could see,' he said with no trace of fear. 'Do you reckon we've hit any of them?'

'Oh, bound to have hit some of them.' Mrs Marsh smiled. 'We've got a flask of tea. Would you like some?'

Griff said they would and tried not to flinch at the noise. How did people stand this, night after night? It was a wonder they weren't all raving mad by now!

He thought of Nell and closed his eyes. Pray God she's all right, he thought.

* * *

In the morning, Ruth made her way to Nell's house, but found her way was blocked.

'Sorry love, you can't come any farther. They've found an unexploded bomb down there.'

Ruth looked along the street which yesterday had been lined with houses on one side, flats on the other. The pub on the corner had gone, so had two of the houses, but the worst damage was to the flats.

Ruth craned her neck in an effort to see, but knew in her heart that one of the flattened houses was Nell's.

The residents had been waiting since they got out of the shelters. They stood in a huddle a few yards away from the barriers and Ruth went over to them.

'Where's Nell?' She recognised one of Nell's neighbours.

'Haven't seen her.' The woman shrugged. 'Anyone see Nell Walker down the shelter?'

Ruth waited as the question went round the waiting people.

'Please.' She went among them. 'Somebody must have seen Nell!'

There was a sudden, awful silence and all eyes turned to the ruined street.

'No,' Ruth said. 'She can't be there . . . she can't! She promised me she'd go down to the shelter.'

Tears clouded her eyes and when she turned, she saw two familiar figures approaching from the other direction. The big, burly shape of Griffith Thomas and the skinny figure of Eddie Walker.

Any other time, she would have been delighted to have seen them, but not now. Not now.

Breaking away from the other people, Ruth ran towards them. Eddie had his gas mask over his shoulder and was carrying the little bag given to him by his Nan.

'Hello, Ruth.' Griff smiled cheerfully. 'I bet you weren't expecting to see us!'

'Mr Thomas . . . Eddie . . . ' Ruth took hold of their arms and made them turn around. She had to spare Eddie the sight of his home in ruins at all costs.

'Someone's got to tell them,' a woman cried out. 'Hey you!' She ran to the barrier and shouted at the men working beyond it and Eddie turned to look at her. Everything slowed down for Ruth as she realised that she could no longer protect the boy from the truth about his beloved nan.

'There's a woman buried under one of those houses! Nell Walker . . . '

'No!' Eddie screamed, tearing himself away from Ruth's grip and flinging himself at the barrier. One of the men held him back, oblivious to his kicking feet and flailing arms.

Ruth took hold of him and wrapped her arms around him so tight that he couldn't move and she held him like that until all the fight went out of him and he became limp against her.

Then she looked up and through a haze of tears saw Jimmy.

'Eddie,' he said softly. 'Eddie, come here, son.'

'Dad!'

Any joy the child felt at seeing his father again was lost, swamped by the grief which tore at his heart as massive sobs racked his small body.

Ruth looked at Griff. The big man was slumped, his head down, his face a mask of pain.

'We can't stay here,' she said, taking charge of these three grief-stricken males. 'We'll go over to my house. Come on, we should be able to get a bus at least part of the way.'

9

Silly old fool, she thought as she hurried down the street. What on earth could she have been thinking of? What a mess to get herself into!

Her face was scratched, there were eleven stitches in a cut on her forearm and she had a terrible headache, but she was still angry with herself.

She stopped dead when she reached the end of her street! Where was the pub? She propelled herself forward on legs which felt suddenly like lead.

The flats . . . the houses . . . her house! There was a massive crater in the middle of the road.

'When did this happen?' She ran to one of the men picking over the rubble of her ruined house.

'Last night, love. I should stand back out of the way if I were you.'

'Well, what are you doing?' Nell said.

'What are you looking for? There was no-one here.'

'I'm afraid there was, love.' The man took her by the arm and led her away to a safe distance. 'The lady of the house — '

'What?' Nell snorted. 'That's me! I am the lady of the house! You're looking for me!' she declared to the stunned man.

She stomped around the piles of bricks as the man, bemused, started to call the rescue operation off. Neighbours who had joined in the search looked up and laughed with relief, but Nell found her way to the back of the house.

There, a man had paused to study a dust-covered photograph. The glass in the frame was broken and he was carefully moving the sliver out of the way.

'Jimmy,' Nell said softly. 'Are you looking for me, love?'

He spun round, dropping the picture.

'Mum!' he yelled, scrambling to his

feet. He hugged her fiercely, then held her away so he could look at her.

'Where have you been? What happened to you?'

'I wasn't going to go to the shelter,' she said shakily. 'I went to bed and everything, but then I kept thinking of Eddie and what would happen to him if anything happened to me . . .

'In the end I got up, dressed and thought I'd find my way to the shelter. But in the blackout, I could hardly see my hand in front of my face and when a bomb went off near where I was walking, I was thrown into a pile of broken glass.

'I was a bit shaken and an ARP warden took me to the hospital . . . They kept me there all day and then I came home and . . . Ruth?'

The colour flooded from her face.

'Ruth wasn't . . . ?'

'No, love.' Jimmy hugged her. 'Ruth's OK.'

'I'm just glad,' Nell said tearfully, 'that our Eddie's safe in Wales.'

Jimmy gave her a look then and she frowned.

'What?'

'He's not in Wales, Mum,' Jimmy said. 'Come on, we'll see if we can salvage anything out of this lot, then I'll take you to Ruth's house. That's where he is right now, with Ruth and Griff.'

'Griff?' Nell cried. 'He's here, too?'

'I think he's come to take you back to Wales.' Jimmy grinned. 'And a good thing, too, if you ask me. I'll be a lot happier about going if I know you're safe.'

'Going?' Nell whispered. 'Going where, Jim?'

'You know I can't tell you that, Mum. But I've got until tomorrow . . . '

The following morning, Jimmy was waiting when Ruth finally came off duty at the ambulance station.

'Who's that?' Jean nudged her. 'Your fellow, is it?'

Ruth blushed. 'Yes,' she said, smiling. 'Yes, I suppose he is.'

'He's nice, isn't he?' Jean laughed. 'But then, show me a man that doesn't look good in a uniform!'

'Oh, Jean!' Ruth laughed.

'Go on, get off with you,' Jean said. 'I'll see you tonight and you can tell me all about him.'

'I haven't long,' Jimmy said as Ruth came over to him. 'Just an hour,'

'An hour!' Ruth cried. 'I thought we had until this afternoon . . . '

'I've said my goodbyes to Mum and Eddie,' he said. 'I don't want to go back to your house. Can we find somewhere quiet to talk?'

'In London?' Ruth laughed ruefully. 'We can try.'

They found the spot they were looking for down by the river, by which time, Jimmy's hour had already dwindled to twenty-five minutes.

He held her hands in his, gazed into her eyes, so clear and bright in her smudged face.

'I want you to go back to Wales,' he said earnestly.

'I can't do that,' she said.

'I thought you'd say that.' He grinned. 'Look, you may not hear from me for some time. I'm going . . . well, it doesn't matter where. The best thing you can do, Ruth, is to forget me.'

'I can't do that either,' she said softly.

'I was hoping you'd say that.' He laughed. 'I love you, Ruth. But promise me, if you meet someone else before I come back . . . don't wait.'

'I'm not going to meet anyone else, Jimmy,' she whispered softly. 'There's only you.'

'If only there was more time,' he said, wrenching his eyes from hers. 'There's so much I want to say to you. Just . . . just look after yourself, Ruth. Be careful and . . . '

'You, too,' she said. 'Oh, Jimmy, you, too.'

They kissed then, a hurried, urgent kiss which had to, by circumstance, end abruptly. He tore himself away from her and rushed off, never turning back.

She watched him go, tears burning

her eyes, waiting until he'd disappeared from sight before turning, walking slowly home, to cousin Rachel's house.

Nell had been busy and had got Eddie and Griff hard at work, too. Ruth hardly recognised the place when she walked in.

She tried to thank Nell, but the older woman waved her hands at her.

'I needed something to do to take my mind off, well, you know. Anyway, it's mainly dust, nothing a damp cloth can't cure! You should get off to bed.' She put the cloth down and touched Ruth's arm. 'I know it's difficult, but try to get some sleep, love.'

Ruth nodded and went upstairs. How lucky they were to have this house . . . But for how long? How long could they withstand Hitler's wrath? How long before this house, too, was reduced to rubble?

The sheets were damp and full of holes, but Ruth's exhaustion was so complete that she did indeed, fall asleep quickly.

Throughout the autumn, the bombing went on and Griff found that his first thoughts, that he'd never be able to stand it, were mistaken. In fact, the more he endured, the more he felt he could face.

Yet there was the farm to be run and it was vitally important that it was run as efficiently as it possibly could. Each egg, each handful of grain, each pint of milk was so important.

He'd turned some of his land over to arable production and was eager to see whether anything would come of it. The land girls were a cheerful, willing bunch, but he wanted to be there with them, working his land, producing the food his country so desperately needed.

He waited until November before asking Nell to marry him and this time, her answer was a clear and confident yes.

It was surprising how quickly a wedding could be arranged. Ruth made

Nell a suit of burgundy-coloured material and friends and neighbours got together to make a wedding cake.

Two weeks before Christmas, 1940, Nell and Griff were married and despite the war, it was a happy occasion for all concerned. Nell looked wonderful, much too young to be grandmother to Eddie, and Griff looked so big and handsome.

David Anderson provided a car for the bride and 'groom and as Jimmy's best friend, stood in on Jimmy's behalf to give the bride away. He was a cheerful, young man, the only indication of the injuries he'd suffered, a pronounced limp.

They had a knees-up afterwards in a local pub which the rector attended, determined to enter into the spirit of things. He was a jolly, old gentleman with white, bushy hair and eyebrows like caterpillars.

Gathered around the piano, voices raised in song, the guests seemed unaware of Ruth sitting alone in the corner. She felt oddly isolated. Jimmy should have been here to share in the happiness and not knowing where he was made the pain all the more acute.

She wasn't alone in that, she knew. Very few people knew the exact whereabouts of their loved ones.

Suddenly, she felt the weight of a hand on her shoulder and turning, looked up to see Nell standing beside her.

'Thinking about Jimmy?' Nell said, sitting down beside Ruth.

Ruth nodded. 'He'd be made up with all this,' she said. 'He'd be even happier if he knew you were going back to Wales with Griff.'

'I know.' Nell smiled. 'I've been thinking about what you've told me. I've decided to go home with Griff, Ruth, and to take Eddie with us. I'd like it very much if you'd come, too.'

'No.' Ruth smiled and shook her head. 'I can't. But I'm glad you've decided to go, very glad.'

'I'm not running out on London

though,' Nell said, frowning. 'I hope you don't think that.'

'Of course not.' Ruth laughed. 'London will still be here after the war. You'll always have your roots here, but you'll be happy in Wales with Griff and Eddie. I know you will.'

Ruth went with them to the station. Cousin Rachel's house was going to seem terribly quiet now without her guests, but she was glad they were leaving. Every night brought fresh waves of destruction and the night before Nell's wedding, Ruth had picked up a boy of Eddie's age who had been badly injured in a raid.

Very gently, she had told Nell about the little boy, knowing that it would tip the scales in favour of her getting out of London.

'Won't you reconsider and come with us?' Nell asked Ruth yet again before they boarded the train. 'You've already done so much here, Ruth . . . let someone else take a turn.'

Ruth shook her head.

'My work isn't finished here yet,' she said. 'But we can still write and I'll get down to see you as often as I can.'

'Then just come with us for Christmas,' Nell pleaded and again Ruth shook her head.

'You will be careful, won't you?' Eddie said.

Ruth looked down and saw that Eddie was gazing up at her, his small face clouded with worry.

'You know I will.' She bent down to hug him and had to bite back the tears. He meant so much to her, this thin, little boy — they all did.

The big, gruff Welshman, the warm, kindly Londoner and most of all, the absent Jimmy. Somehow, they'd become the family she'd lost so long ago, filling the gap in her heart to the edges.

The guard blew his whistle and began to slam the doors shut along the train. Griff hurried Nell and Eddie on to the train, then turned to speak to Ruth.

'You know where we are if you need anything,' he said. 'Anything at all, Ruth. You've been good to us, letting us stay with you and helping with the wedding and everything.'

He stooped to kiss her cheek, then got on the train and pulled the door shut behind him.

Ruth stood on the platform, waving until the train had gone, then turning, she hurried home to the empty house.

10

Over the weeks and months that followed, Ruth put Cousin Rachel's house to good use, providing a home for homeless families. Her days and nights were full, so full that she hardly ever noticed the passage of time and only occasionally allowed her thoughts to wander to Jimmy.

The relentless bombing of London finally dwindled after months, but there was still to be no rest. They had been prepared to handle thousands of military casualties, but the number of civilians killed and injured far exceeded estimates.

Months became years and Ruth heard nothing of Jimmy until one day in the late summer of '43 when a telegram arrived for Nell Walker.

She stared at it. Nell Walker . . . Nell Thomas now and living all those miles away in Wales.

She couldn't open it up, couldn't send it on.

There was only one thing she could do because she had to know what was inside it. She'd have to take it to Wales herself . . .

Ruth stood at the foot of the hill and took in a deep breath. How unchanged it all was here, how beautiful and calm and welcoming. It was almost possible to forget the reason for her mission beneath these cloudless, blue skies.

She'd become so used to looking up at a sky dotted with barrage balloons, at smashed streets, at men and women in tin hats dragging people from piles of rubble, at banners and posters supporting the war efforts, at uniforms on every corner that normality came as a shock.

As she made her way towards Thomas's farm, she saw that he'd turned a great many of his fields over to crop production and that young women laughed and joked as they worked. She'd heard so much about the Land

Army, had seen film of them on the newsreels and here they were for real.

Walking into the yard, she saw Nell at once. A slimmer, healthier-looking Nell with rosy cheeks and her grey hair now cut fashionably short. She looked up, sensing Ruth's approach and with a little cry of joy, dropped what she was doing and rushed over to her.

'Ruth! How lovely to see you . . . and about time, too! Will you stay? How are you? Oh, you do look pale, dear, was the journey very harrowing? How are things in London? You must tell me what's been happening . . . '

She linked her arm through Ruth's and together they walked into the kitchen. Griff had his head bowed over accounting books and as soon as he saw Ruth, he knew that she had come bearing bad news. Nell, blinded by her joy at seeing Ruth, had failed to see the sadness in the girl's eyes.

He got up, kissed her cheek, but his eyes betrayed his fear for Nell.

'I'll make some tea,' he said.

'You haven't said a word yet,' Nell rattled on cheerfully.

'Nell, I . . . ' Ruth began. There really was no easy way to deal with this, no way of softening the blow. Better to get it over and done with right away.

She opened her handbag and took out the telegram.

'I haven't read it,' she murmured.

Nell stared at it for a moment, wide-eyed, her face paling. Griff left the tea and came over to place his huge paw of a hand on her shoulder.

'Shall I . . . ?' he said.

'No,' she whispered. 'It must be me.'

After what seemed an eternity, she picked it up, opened it. Ruth's heart was drumming behind her ribs. All this time that telegram had been in her bag and she had been aching to know what was inside. It didn't always have to be bad news.

She watched as Nell's eyes skimmed across the words, the rigid expression on her face never changing, giving nothing away until the moment when she closed her eyes tight shut and tears began to trickle out from between her clenched lids.

Griff looked at Ruth, saw the agony of waiting, the pain she was still enduring.

'Missing in action,' he said and with those three simple words, conveyed a message of hope . . .

★ ★ ★

'Ruth?' Richard emerged from the school gates, his eyes brightening at the sight of her. 'When did you get back? How are you? You look frightful.'

'I came to meet Eddie,' she said. 'How has he settled down with you?'

'Very well so far.' Richard smiled. 'He's a bright enough boy and has plenty of friends. But Ruth, I couldn't believe it when I looked out of the window and saw you standing here.'

'I had to come,' she said. 'I had a telegram for Nell. Her son, Jimmy . . . he's missing.'

166

'Oh.' Richard sighed. 'I'm so sorry, Ruth, so very sorry. I expect she's taken the news badly?'

'Well . . . ' Ruth said. 'I'm going to make a few calls when I get back to London, let them know of Nell's re-marriage and her new address so that if . . . when there is any news, she should get it straight away.'

'How long are you staying?' Richard said. 'Would you be able to come and have dinner with us?'

'Us?'

'Marie and I.' He grinned bashfully. 'We were married last spring.'

'Oh, Richard, I'm so pleased for you,' Ruth said. 'But I'll be leaving first thing in the morning, so . . . so perhaps another time. In the meantime, give Marie my love and tell her . . . tell her that she's married one of the best!'

'I will.' He smiled, then his eyes darkened. 'I could let Eddie out early today,' he said. 'You'll want to tell him . . . ?'

'Yes, Nell wants me to talk to him,'

she said. 'She seems to think he'll take the news better from me.'

Ruth suspected the real reason was that Nell couldn't trust herself not to break down in front of him.

When he came out of the school gates, Ruth hardly recognised him. His mouth seemed full of big, strong teeth and he had grown so tall that he matched her own height. He was stick thin, like most of the boys his age, but his limbs had a firm strength which told of a big man in years to come.

'Miss Lewis!' He grinned, made to hug her, then pulled back just in time, with a backward glance at the school. He was at an awkward age when displays of affection had to be carried out with the utmost care.

Ruth held out her hand to shake his.

'Ruth, call me Ruth, now, Eddie. We've been too close for formalities.'

'Mr Noble let me out early as you were here,' Eddie said. 'Why did you come after all this time? Is it something to do with my dad?'

They walked on a little way, then Ruth stopped and took hold of his arm.

'Your nan has had a telegram,' she said. 'Your dad is missing in action. Do you understand what that means, Eddie?'

He stared at her, those blue eyes still a child's yet possessing an understanding which went far beyond his years.

Eventually he nodded.

'He's probably dead,' he said flatly.

'Not necessarily,' she said. 'We can't give up on him, Eddie.'

'No.' He smiled. There were no tears, no show of emotions whatsoever and Ruth realised that Eddie, of all of them, had probably come to terms with this years ago.

'How are things in London?'

She welcomed his change of subject and was relieved that he didn't fall apart at the news about his father. At the same time, she wished he wouldn't bottle up his feelings.

'Not so bad,' she said. 'I'm working as a teacher again. Lots of children have come back and I've actually some evacuees from some of the east coast ports in my class! I still drive an ambulance as well.'

'I wish I were older,' Eddie said vehemently. 'I can't wait until I'm old enough to fight.'

'Oh, Eddie,' Ruth cried. 'I hope that by the time you are old enough, the war will be over!'

He flashed her a look of pure hatred, but the hate was not for her, but for those who had started the war.

'I hope not,' he said, clenching his fists.

★　★　★

The months passed and no more news came of Jimmy. Griff watched miserably as Nell grew thin with worry. If only there were some word, one way or another.

They heard from Ruth about the V1s, buzz bombs that had started to drop in the summer of 1944.

'They're *worse than the ordinary bombs*, she wrote. *You hear the buzz and know as long as you can hear it, you'll be all right, then it stops and you hold your breath and wait and wait because you know then that it's only a matter of seconds before it lands. I'm back on the ambulances full-time again now . . .*'

'Must be dreadful,' Nell said, folding the letter Griff had just read. 'Poor Ruth.'

'At least she still has her home,' Griff said. 'It seems to have escaped damage.'

'She says they don't even bother to have warnings when the buzz bombs are coming.' Nell sighed. 'And they're in and out of the shelters half the time.'

'He's getting desperate, Nell,' Griff said. 'He knows he can't break our spirit and he's getting desperate.'

There came a knock at the door, interrupting their conversation and Griff answered to find a young man, a petty officer in the Royal Navy standing outside.

Nell got up, came to stand behind Griff.

'I'm Peter Thomas,' the young man said, sweeping his hat off his head and revealing red-blond hair, cut brutally short.

'Peter?' Griff gasped. 'My Peter . . . ?'

'Come in.' Nell pulled him into the kitchen in case he should decide to run off.

'I wasn't sure if you'd want to see me,' Peter explained. 'It's been so long.'

'Of course I wanted to see you,' Griff said tearfully. 'If only you knew how I'd longed to see you. Oh, this is my wife, Nell . . . we were married in London four years ago.'

His smile was proud as he introduced them.

'This is my son, Nell . . . *my son*.'

Peter smiled at Nell. 'That makes you my stepmother,' he said.

'Have you any news of the others?' Griff asked eagerly. 'It's been so long . . . I can't believe . . . '

'David's in the navy, too,' Peter said.

'And Lily's a Wren! So you could say we're all at sea! Except Lily of course, who is a switchboard operator, but just as important as anyone!'

Nell made a pot of tea and stood it on the table between the two men, father and son.

'I'm going to walk down to see if I can see Eddie around,' she said, looking for an excuse to leave.

'You don't have to go,' Griff said.

'I know.' She smiled and left anyway.

She was so happy for Griff, that his son had sought him out after all this time and had brought news, good news of his other children, but her happiness was tinged with regret.

If only there were some news of Jimmy. She stopped and gazed up at the white, fluffy clouds gathered in the sky. She hadn't lost hope, but it was so difficult to cling to it and she knew that if he was dead, then she'd rather know than live through this agony of uncertainty.

By the time she got back to the

farmhouse, Griff's son had gone.

'He couldn't stay,' Griff said gruffly.

'He's a fine young man,' Nell said. 'You must be very proud.'

'No more proud than you are of Jimmy,' he said and when she looked into the golden pools of his eyes, she knew he understood what she was going through.

★　★　★

Ruth stumbled along the street which was alive with people and song. Even the sun was shining brilliantly as though in celestial celebration of the victory in Europe.

She'd been sleeping and had woken to the sound of joyful voices which had drawn her out into the street and the throng of people.

Disbelief stunned her. It was over, the war was over and everyone was so happy. She heard a strange noise and realised it was her own laughter, bubbling out. An American GI grabbed her and whirled her round, then kissed her before smiling warmly and letting her go on her way.

Gradually, the reality sunk in and she put her heart and soul into celebrating the day, the eighth of May, finding friends, dancing, singing, until after dark, she found herself in a packed church giving quiet thanks.

And only later, much, much later, did she find herself in the church with just a few others. They had celebrated the end of the war, the beginning of a new life, but had yet to pray for those who would never return to share in the victory and those who were still missing.

Jimmy among them. A man she had known so briefly, yet loved so intensely.

★　★　★

The boy celebrating his twelfth birthday was a far cry from the skinny, pale little lad who'd arrived in the valley with the first wave of evacuees. He was much taller for a start, having put a spurt on in the past twelve months and his teeth were strong and white.

He spoke with a strange accent, a combination of cockney and Welsh and his fair hair had darkened to a shade nearer to that of his father's. The father he hadn't seen since 1940.

Richard Noble sat at the table with the boys. Eddie had particularly asked that no girls should be invited to this party, but had wanted his new teacher to attend.

He looked up and saw the farmer watching him. The boys were laughing and talking amongst themselves and Richard thought that there was much for them to be happy about. The war with Germany was over after six years, the threat to their homeland gone. He got up from the table and went to stand beside Griff.

'There can't be many left to go back now,' Griff said thoughtfully. A lot of the evacuees had drifted back home over the years of the war. Some when they were fourteen, others sooner, when their parents sent for them.

'I think you can safely say that any left here are here for good,' Richard said.

Nell nodded and turned to Ruth, who had come to Wales especially for Eddie's birthday. The two women shared something in the loss of Jimmy, a bond which drew them close.

Marie, pregnant and blooming, turned to smile radiantly at Richard.

'I'm a little tired,' she said. 'Would you mind if I took the car, Richard?'

'You'll do no such thing! Driving in your condition! I'll take you home and we'll drop some of these boys off on the way. You won't mind if we leave now, Griff?'

Griff said nothing, but smiled wanly.

'You do feel all right, don't you?' Richard frowned at his young wife.

She laughed. 'Why shouldn't I?' And turned to Nell. 'I find everything so wearying, carrying all this weight around with me!'

Nell laughed, too, laughter tinged

with sadness. She had only known the joy of childbirth once and that child was lost to her, man that he was now.

The Nobles left then, taking the boys with them, leaving just the family at the farm. They came outside into the yard to wave at the car, filled to bursting with singing, laughing boys.

Nell and Griff were first to go in, then Ruth was left alone with Eddie.

'Are you coming in?'

'Not just yet,' he said, seeming so grown up now. 'I just want to be on my own for a bit.'

Ruth nodded and went inside. Yes, it was hitting many people like that now that the initial joy was over. For some people, this war would never end.

It was a mark of his maturity that he needed time to be on his own.

Eddie walked to the edge of the yard, where the lane began and rhododendrons flowered in abundance. It was ironic that he could remember more birthdays spent here than anywhere else. He felt so strongly that he belonged here, yet London beckoned him and he knew that one day, he would have to return to that city he called home.

Everything was coming into leaf, pale, delicate greens heralding the brand newness of another season.

He held his breath, hearing movement in the lane. One of his mates, come back to play a birthday trick? He was ready for them. He leaped from the gateway so that he stood in the middle of the lane and saw none of his friends, but a man approaching.

A man, thin and tired, with blue-blue eyes and a broad grin which dimpled his pale cheeks.

Eddie's jaw dropped as he stood, braced for anything, anything in the world but this.

'Dad . . . ' he gasped at last.

'Hello, son . . . '

'Nan.' Eddie entered the kitchen, appearing calm, but his flushed cheeks telling a different story.

'What's happened, love?' Nell left the

washing up. 'You've gone all pink!'

'Can you come outside a minute?' Eddie said. 'I want to show you something . . .'

Laughing, Nell followed him.

'What are you up to Eddie? I've got all this washing up to do . . .'

'I'll finish this,' Ruth said, taking over the washing up. 'I don't know how eight boys can make such a mess,' she said to Griff.

He shrugged, put the tea cloth down and walked slowly to the window. Outside in the yard, he saw the young man appear as if from nowhere, saw Nell run to embrace him and felt a lump form in his throat so big he could hardly breathe.

'Jimmy,' he whispered to himself. 'Thank God, thank God.'

Forgetting Ruth, he went outside where Nell was tearfully hugging her son, kissing him, sobbing six years worth of news between gulping breaths.

'He's been with the resistance fighters,' Eddie said proudly.

'There was no way of getting word to you that I was still alive,' Jimmy said apologetically. 'I was taken prisoner and the convoy we were being moved in was bombed. I managed to get away in the confusion and . . . I've been trying to get back home ever since, but there always seemed to be something to do. In the end, there was nothing I could do, but await the liberation!'

'I thought you were dead,' Nell cried accusingly.

'There were times when I thought so, too,' Jimmy said, putting his arm around her shoulders.

'I went to London, found Ruth's house full of strangers, so I went to the garage where David told me that you'd married Griff. It's a bit late.' He held out his hand to shake Griff's. 'But congratulations all the same!'

The draining-board was becoming full since Griff had dropped his tea cloth to go wandering off outside. Ruth wiped her arm across her forehead as steam from the water wafted in her face, making her hot.

She heard the door open and close behind her.

'About time, too.' She laughed. 'I thought you'd all deserted me! Someone had better get on with this drying up before it all falls back into the sink!'

She plunged her hands back into the water as someone took up the cloth and picked up a plate.

She looked at the hand first. Too small for Griff, too big for Eddie, too masculine for Nell.

With a little cry, she dropped the plate she was washing into the sink and, turning, found herself standing right beside Jimmy.

He put the plate down and she blinked, half convinced she was seeing things.

'Jimmy?' she whispered eventually.

'Yes,' he said softly. 'I'm real. I'm back.'

She flung her arms around him then, her cry of joy breaking into a sob as tears streamed down her face. She pushed him away so she could look at him, touched his face, his hands, convincing herself he was really there.

'I told you not to wait,' he admonished lightly.

'But I did.' She laughed. 'I did wait, Jimmy, and I'm glad.'

'So am I,' he said, then pulling her into his arms and holding her as though he'd never let her go, he kissed her.

Ruth's war was, at last, over.

THE END

We do hope that you have enjoyed reading this large print book.

Did you know that all of our titles are available for purchase?

We publish a wide range of high quality large print books including:
Romances, Mysteries, Classics
General Fiction
Non Fiction and Westerns

Special interest titles available in large print are:
The Little Oxford Dictionary
Music Book, Song Book
Hymn Book, Service Book

Also available from us courtesy of Oxford University Press:
Young Readers' Dictionary
(large print edition)
Young Readers' Thesaurus
(large print edition)

For further information or a free brochure, please contact us at:
Ulverscroft Large Print Books Ltd.,
The Green, Bradgate Road, Anstey,
Leicester, LE7 7FU, England.
Tel: (00 44) 0116 236 4325
Fax: (00 44) 0116 234 0205

HEARTS IN EXILE

Catriona McCuaig

Two teachers are evacuated from Coventry to the Welsh countryside, where they struggle with wartime hardship as they help their pupils adjust to a different way of life. Will love follow them there? Vivacious Tansy sees marriage as a way to escape her impoverished background, while shy Dinah just wants to find someone to love. She falls for handsome Emlyn, but the young Welshman is equally reserved. How will they ever get together?